DIC

MW00415741

TERMS   MUSICIANS

THEORY

WILLIAM F. LEE III, PH.D, MUS.D
PROFESSOR OF MUSIC
DEAN, COLLEGE OF FINE ARTS AND HUMANITIES
UNIVERSITY OF TEXAS AT SAN ANTONIO

TABLE OF CONTENTS

ABBREVIATIONS OF FOREIGN LANGUAGES

Arabic	Arab.
Chinese	Chi.
French	Fr.
German	Ger.
Greek	Gr.
Hebrew	Heb.
Hindi	Hin.
Hungarian	Hun.
Indian	In.
Italian	It.
Japanese	Jap.
Korean	Kor.
Latin	Lat.
Norwegian	Norw.
Old English	Old Eng.
Polish	Pol.
Portuguese	Port.
Russian	Rus.
Sanskrit	Sans.
Spanish	Sp.

TERMS

Aa

A *(It.)* To, from, by. *(Sp.)* To, at, in, by, of. In the diatonic major scale of C, A is the sixth tone.

A & R - In the recording business, A means artist, R, repertory.

A 440 (acoustics) - a1, equal to 440 vibrations per second, is unanimously adopted as the standard pitch.

Absolute music - Music composed completely for music's sake without reference to non-musical implications.

Absolute Pitch - A highly developed ability to quickly compare an audible impression with acoustic archetypes stored in the memory.

Absorption (acoustics) - The weakening of sound waves through incomplete reflection.

A cappella *(It.)* Unaccompanied.

Accelerando *(It.)* Becoming faster.

Accent *(Fr.)* The stress of one tone over others. Expression.

Accentor - A performer who sings or plays the leading part; sometimes signifies the conductor or director.

Accessory tone - See nonharmonic tone.

Acciaccatura *(It.)* A short accented appoggiature. *See* **THEORY - MUSICAL ORNAMENTS.**

Accidentals - Music symbols placed at the left side of the head of a note to raise, lower, or return to normal the pitch of a note. Ex: sharp (#); flat (♭); natural (♮); double sharp (x); double flat (♭♭).

Accompaniment - The separate, secondary part or parts that accompany the principal solo in any composition.

Accorder *(Fr.)* To tune.

Accordion - A music instrument, the tone of which is produced by the inspiration and respiration of a pair of bellows acting upon metallic reeds.

Acetate - An individually pressed record. Songwriters use acetates to interest publishers and record companies in their songs.

Acoustic guitar - A guitar with a resonating sound box that uses nylon or steel strings and is non-electric.

Acoustics - The science dealing with sound and the treatment thereof.

Acoustic bass - Organ stop with two rows of pipes. Also, a double bass.

Acoustic suspension speaker - A speaker or system of speakers sealed in an air-tight chamber, which widens the frequency range by allowing a good bass response in a small enclosure.

Adagio *(It.)* A slow tempo, between andante and lento.

ADC *(A/D converter)* - Analog to digital converter. A device which takes in analog (electrical) information and converts it to numeric (digital) information.

Added sixth - The sixth added to a triad. *See* **THEORY - CHORD TYPES.**

A deux *(Fr.)* For two instruments or voices.

Ad libitum *(Lat.)* Improvised; freely, at will.

ADST - A module which is present in all synthesizers meaning attack, decay, sustain, and release.

A due *(or a2) (It.)* For two instruments or voices. Used to indicate that two instruments, playing from the same part, are to play in unison.

Aeolian harp - A stringed instrument so constructed as to give forth musical sounds when exposed to a current of air.

Aeolian mode - The same as the natural minor scale or descending melodic minor. *See* **THEORY - SCALES AND MODES.**

Affabile *(It.)* Gentle, pleasing.

A.F.M. - The American Federation of Musicians. The national union which represents all professional musicians in the United States and Canada.

Agitato *(It.)* Restless, excited.

Agogic accent - An accent effected not by dynamic stress or by higher pitch, but by longer duration of the note.

Air - Tune, melody.

Air de cour *(Fr.)* A short strophic song.

Air waves (acoustics) - Waves which are produced by any disturbance or by something which is vibrating in only one line of motion.

Alberti bass - Idiomatic figures of accompaniment for the left hand in keyboard music, consisting of broken chords.

Aleatory music - Music that has elements of chance in either the composition or the performance. Often called "chance music."

Al fine *(It.)* To the end.

Algorithm - A mathematical term which in music applies when any special species of notation or calculation is developed toward a particular musical realization in sound.

Alla breve *(It.)* Originally 4/2 meter, each measure being equal to a breve, or double whole note. Now usually 2/2 meter (¢).

Allargando *(It.)* Slowing down, becoming broader and sometimes also louder.

Allegretto *(It.)* Moderately quick tempo, between andante and allegro.

Allegro *(It.)* Fast, lively tempo, between allegretto and presto.

Allemande *(Fr.)* A German dance in 3/4 meter, like the Landler.

Alliteration - A group of words beginning with the same letter.

Al segno *(It.)* Return to the sign.

Alteration - The raising or lowering of a note by means of a sharp or flat, thereby altering the chord structure.

Altered chord - A diatonic chord that has been altered by raising or lowering one or more of its elements (root, third, fifth, or seventh) a half step but has not changed the tonality.

Alto *(Fr.)* **Viola** *(It.)* High; in former times a high part above the tenor, now applied to the lowest female voices.

Alto clef - Usually used by the viola player in modern notation. Third line indicates c1. *See* **THEORY - CLEFS**.

American Society of Composers, Authors and Publishers - *See* **ASCAP**.

American Symphony Orchestra League *(ASOL)* - A nonprofit research and service organization. Voting memberships are held by arts councils and symphony orchestras.

Amplifier - An electronic device that alters the amplitude or intensity of a signal.

Amplitude (acoustics) - The difference between the high and low phases of a sound wave or sound cycle. Usually expressed in pressure as it affects the ear drum; determines the loudness of sound.

Anacrusis *(Ger.)* Another term for upbeat which indicates a melody or notes beginning with an incomplete measure.

Analog - An electronic signal whose waveform resembles that of the original signal.

Analog computer - An automatic electronic calculating machine that solves problems and processes data to represent numerical variables.

Analog synthesizers - Synthesizers that produce sound by electronic means. Computers produce sound digitally, which is the numeric representation of sound.

Analyzing - The process of recognizing the relation of structural details of a unified whole. It is primarily recognition of design.

Andante *(It.)* A moderately slow tempo between adagio and allegretto.

Andantino *(It.)* Slightly faster than andante.

Animato *(It.)* Animated, spirited, lively.

Antecedent - The first phrase of a period or announcing phrase. *See* **Period**.

Anthem - A composition for voices, with or without instrumental accompaniment, enjoined by the ritual of the Anglican Church.

Anticipation - A nonharmonic tone which might be considered the opposite of a suspension. It is sounded in the melody before the chord in which it fits is heard. *See* **THEORY - NONHARMONIC TONES.**

Antiphonal - In the style of an antiphon. A collection of antiphons.

Appoggiatura *(It.)* A melodic ornament. The accented (long) appoggiatura, written as a small note, is accented and borrows time value from the note it precedes. The short appoggiatura (grace note) is usually written as a small eighth or sixteenth note with a slanting stroke through the hook and stem. A non-chord tone usually located in a metrically strong position. *See* **THEORY - MUSICAL ORNAMENTS, NONHARMONIC TONES.**

Arabic numerals - Figures used to identify scale degrees. Ex: 1, 2, 3, 4, 5, 6, 7. Also used to identify inversions of triads and seventh chords.

Arco *(It.)* The bow, use of the bow; neck of a harp.

Aria *(It.)* An Air, a song, a tune; sung by a single voice either with or without an accompaniment.

Arioso *(It.)* An expressive vocal style, melodic, singing.

Arpeggio *(It.)* Notes played in succession rather than together, a broken chord. *See* **THEORY - SIGNS.**

Arrangement - The adaptation of a composition for instruments other than those for which it was originally written. Music which has been transferred from one medium to another. In jazz, an arrangement is sometimes called a chart.

Arranger - One who transfers music from one medium to another.

Ars antiqua *(Lat.)* A contrapuntal, sometimes dissonant style of 12th-13th century France.

Ars nova *(Lat.)* 14th-century music which contrasted with Ars antiqua through the use of more complex counterpoint.

Articulation - In performance, the clear and distinct rendering of the tones; the art of distinct pronunciation.

Artificial Rhythmic Groupings - *See* **THEORY - ARTIFICIAL RHYTHMIC GROUPINGS**

Art song - A song of serious artistic intent, as distinct from a folk song.

ASCAP - American Society of Composers, Authors, and Publishers. A society founded in 1914 by Victor Herbert to protect copyrights and performing rights.

A tempo *(It.)* Return to the original speed.

A-thematic music - Music which is not based on thematic or motific consistency, but music in which the course develops freely without using the affinity of thematic shapes as a structural bond.

Atonality - Absence of a tonal center.

Attacca *(It.)* Continue without a pause.

Attack - Promptness and decision in beginning a phrase. In electronic music, those amplitude (volume) characteristics at the beginning of a sound.

Audition - Evaluating a performance for student or professional placement or employment; the faculty of hearing.

Augmentation - The lengthening of note values in a melodic line.

Augmented - Raised.

Augmented interval - A perfect interval that is made a half-step larger. *See* **THEORY - INTERVALS.**

Augmented sixth chord - A chord created by use of the minor sixth degree and the chromatically raised fourth degree. *See* **THEORY - SIXTH CHORDS.**

Authentic cadence - The cadence composed of the progression from dominant to tonic harmonies.

Author's harmony - The usage by a composer of another composer's harmonic progression.

Auxiliary tones - Non-harmonic tones which leave a chord tone stepwise and return immediately to the same chord tone. Often referred to as neighboring tones. *See* **THEORY - NONHARMONIC TONES.**

Bb

B - The seventh note of the Scale of C major. In German, B-flat.

Baby grand - The smallest sized grand piano.

Back beat - A secondary rhythmic accent.

Background music - Music written for films to enhance the action or create a particular mood. Also, music arranged in such a manner as to be unobtrusive to the listener, e.g., Muzak and 3M.

Background singers - Frequently vocal groups are used in recording sessions to "back up" solo singers.

Back-up musician - A musician who plays the music for a featured singer or act.

Bagatelles *(Fr.)* Sketches, short pieces, trifles.

Balalaika *(Rus.)* Russian triangular guitar with three strings tuned in fourths.

Balance - In four-part writing, the art of harmonically spacing all voices. In performance, proper balancing between vocal or instrumental voices.

Ballad - A song, short and simple, designed to suit a popular audience. Usually in a descriptive form.

Ballade *(Ger.)* **Ballata** *(It.)* Originally a dance tune. In instrumental music it may be as elaborate as a Chopin "Ballade."

Ballet *(Fr.)* A pantomine story with musical accompaniment. A musical production which utilizes dancers and instrumental music. A composition.

Ballo *(It.)* Dance, in dance tempo.

Band - A number of instrumental performers playing together, usually consisting of the woodwinds, brass, and percussion sections. In wind ensembles sometimes a double bass (string) is added.

Band man - A jazzman who excels in ensemble playing, though is not necessarily a distinguished soloist.

Band master - The leader or conductor of a band.

Banjo - A five-stringed instrument with long neck, whose sound is reinforced by a parchment covered hoop.

Bar - Measure.

Barbershop harmony - Close harmony, with chromatic passing notes, which American singing barbers made popular in the early 1900's.

Bar line - A line drawn from the top to the bottom of a staff to denote the division of the meter in a piece of music.

Barcarola *(It.)* **Barcarolle** *(Fr.)* A song or air sung by the Venetian gondoliers, usually in 6/8 meter.

Baritone - Bariton *(Fr.)* **Baritone** *(It.)* A male voice between the bass and tenor.

Baritone horn - A transposing instrument with music usually written in the bass clef (although beginners sometimes learn in the treble clef), which sounds a ninth lower than written. The four-valve baritone horn is called a euphonium.

Bar-lines - Lines dividing a certain number of beats into measures. The bar-line also indicates the position of the main accent.

Barn dance - An American dance of rural origin taking its name from the festivities usual in the building of a new barn.

Baroque music - Music of the period 1600 - 1750.

Bass *(Ger.)* In music composition, the lowest of the parts. The lowest male voice. An acoustic or electric instrument of four strings tuned E, A, D, and G.

Bass clarinet - The bass instrument of the clarinet family whose range is an octave below that of the B♭ clarinet.

Bass clef - The F clef on the fourth line. *See* **THEORY - CLEFS**.

Bass drum - The lowest pitched and largest drum of indefinite pitch.

Basso *(It.)* Bass voice or part.

Basso continuo *(It.)* A guide to the harmonic background of the keyboard music in order to fill-in missing parts or to reinforce weak ones. The continual or figured bass in 18th-century music. See figured bass.

Bassoon - A woodwind instrument of the oboe or double reed family.

Basso ostinato *(It.)* A short bass figure, one or two measures in length, which is repeated continuously throughout a passage or composition.

Bass trombone - The trombone with practical range from C below the bass staff to the E above.

Bass trumpet - A trumpet pitched an octave lower than the B♭ trumpet.

Bass tuba - A brass intrument of low pitch with a compass of four octaves.

Batterie *(Fr.)* Percussion section; drum roll.

Battuta *(It.)* Measure, bar, beat.

Beam - Used in place of flags to show the groups of notes which are to be sung on one syllable. In instrumental music, beams are used to group notes into metric patterns. *See* **THEORY - SIGNS**.

Beat - The temporal unit of a composition, as is indicated by the up-and-down movements of the conductor's hand. An acoustical phenomenon resulting from the interference of two sound waves of slightly different frequency.

Be bop - A complex style of jazz which began in the early 1940's associated with Charlie Parker and Dizzy Gillespie.

Bel canto *(It.)* Literally "well sung." A pure and sympathetic   legato, the opposite of bravura, coloratur, agilita, etc.

Bell - The lower termination of any tubular musical instrument which assumes the form of a bell.

Bellows - A pneumatic appendage for supplying organ pipes with air.

Bells - Orchestral glockenspiel or the chimes.

Belly - The piano soundboard. The upper side of the resonant box of violins, lutes, etc.

Berceuse *(Fr.)* Lullaby.

Bewegt *(Ger.)* Animated, with motion.

Bichord - Two strings. Bichord instruments include the mandolin, lute, and certain pianos having a pair of strings, for each tone, tuned in unison.

Big band - A large jazz band of twelve to thirty players consisting of woodwinds, brass, and rhythm instruments.

Binary form - Music which is divided into two parts.

Binary measure - Two beats to a measure.

Bird - In jazz, nickname for Charlie Parker (1920-1955), saxophonist, and one of the most influential instrumentalists in the history of jazz.

Bitonality - Use of two different keys at the same time in a composition.

Black bottom - A roaring twenties rapid ballroom dance characterized by sinuous hip movements.

Block chords - Dense chords that usually move in parallel motion. A jazz piano style.

Blowhole - The mouth hole in the flute.

Bluegrass - Kentucky folk music played on the banjo and other stringed instruments and characterized by an unaffected rhythmic quality.

Blue note - In jazz and blues, the lowered third, fifth, and seventh degrees in a major scale.

Blues - In 4/4 meter, an Afro-American, jazz-associated, 12-measure harmonic pattern, utilizing blue notes and soulful lyrics.

BMI - See Broadcast Music Incorporated.

Board - See console.

Board fade - In recording, diminishing the sound on a tape.

Bolero *(Sp.)* Spanish dance in 3/4 meter, also called Cachuca.

Bongos - Hand-held Cuban drums, in pairs, struck by the fingertips.

Boogie woogie - Type of jazz originating from the piano and characterized by ostinato bass figures.

Bop - *See* **Be Bop.**

Bossa nova - "New voice" in Portuguese. Brazilian dance music influenced by jazz.

Bouche *(Fr.)* Mouth. Closed, applied either in vocal music to ask for humming with closed mouth, or in instrumental music as, for example, stopped Horn. Stopped note.

Bourdon *(Fr.)* A sympathetic string, refrain, or bagpipe drone. A flute stope in organs. The carillon's largest bell.

Bourree *(Fr.)* An old French dance.

Bow - A contrivance of wood and horsehair, employed to set the strings of the violin, etc., in vibration.

Bowing - The art of using the bow; playing with the bow. "The bowing" also refers to the marks used to guide the player.

Brace - A figure used to connect two or more staves which are to be performed together. *See* **THEORY - SIGNS**.

Brass band - A performing group consisting of only brass and percussion instruments.

Brass instruments - Trumpet, cornet, bugle, trombone, tuba, French horn, baritone horn, euphonium, sousaphone.

Bravura, con *(It.)* With great technical skill.

Breath mark - A sign indicating that the player or singer may breath at that point. *See* **THEORY - SIGNS**.

Breit *(Ger.)* Broad, broadly.

Breve *(It.)* Concise, brief, short pause. Originally meaning a note equal to two whole notes. *See* **THEORY - NOTATION.**

Bridge - A piece of wood which, on instruments having a sound-board or resonance box, performs the double duty of raising the strings and at terminating at one end their vibrating portion. In jazz, the B section of the ternary ABA form. The bridge is often called the release.

Brio, con *(It.)* With fire, vigorously.

Broadcast Music Inc. - B.M.I. An American performing rights society, founded in 1939, comparable with ASCAP but owned by the broadcasting industry.

Broken chords, broken octaves - Chords or octaves whose notes are played in succession and not simultaneously.

Buffo *(It.)* Comic; a singer who takes comic parts.

Bugle - A brass horn of straight or curved form. Generally used for infantry calls.

Burgundian School - During the Medieval Period, a main center of musical activity.

Burlesque - An extravaganza tending to excite laughter by farcical representations.

Byzantine music - The music of the liturgical chant of the Eastern Orthodox Churches.

Cc

C - The first note in the scale of C. The sign for common time (4/4) is not really a C (Tempus imperfectum), but two-thirds of a circle.

Cable television - A television system in which signals are transmitted by cable rather than by radio waves.

Caccia *(It.)* 14th-century Italian music in two-voice canon.

Cacophony - Harshness, dissonance.

Cadence - A close in melody or harmony ending a period, section or entire piece. The chord progression at the close of a phrase. See Authentic cadence, Perfect authentic cadence, Imperfect authentic cadence, Half cadence, Deceptive cadence, Plagal cadence, Perfect plagal cadence, Imperfect plagal cadence, and Phrygian cadence.

Cadenza *(It.)* A cadenza, florid; cadence, close. An ornamental solo passage introduced near the end of a composition either written by the composer or extemporized by the performer. An extended section in free improvisatory style giving the player or singer a chance to exhibit his technical brilliance.

Cakewalk - A folk dance in ragtime rhythm developed in America.

Calando *(It.)* Becoming slower and softer.

Calliope - An American instrument invented in the 1880's consisting of a number of steam-blown whistles played from a keyboard.

Calmando *(It.)* Subsiding, quieting down.

Calmato *(It.)* Tranquil, quiet.

Calore, con *(It.)* With warmth, impetuous, fervent.

Cambiata *(It.)* An interpolated tone between a dissonant tone, or tendency tone, and its resolution. *See* **THEORY - NONHARMONIC TONES**.

Camel walk - A jazz dance in which shoulder and back movements simulate somewhat those of a camel.

Camera *(It.)* Chamber.

Camerata *(It.)* Small schools in the 16th-century.

Canon - Musical imitation in the strictest form. A strict and extended application of the stretto principle. It may occur at any pitch or rhythmic interval.

Canon crancrizan (Crab canon) - A canon in which voices are sounded forward and backward simultaneously. Also referred to as a retrograde canon.

Cantabile *(It.)* Lyrical, melodious, flowing, in a singing style.

Cantare *(It.)* To sing; to celebrate.

Cantata *(It.)* Vocal work with instrumental accompaniment, shorter than an oratorio.

Canto *(It.)* Song, singing. Soprano or vocal part.

Cantor - A singer, a chanter.

Cantus firmus *(Lat.)* Fixed melody; frequently used as a thematic basis for polyphonic works through the 18th century.

Canzone *(It.)* A song, folk-song; also a part-song in madrigal style.

Cappella *(It.)* A chapel or church. A musical band.

Capriccio *(It.)* Instrumental music in free form.

Capriccioso *(It.)* Freely, fanciful.

Capstan - The driven spindle or shaft in a tape recorder which rotates against the tape.

Carillon *(Fr.)* In organs, a mixture stop. Glockenspiel. A set of bells in a tower played by a keyboard or a mechanism.

Carillons *(Fr.)* Chimes. A set of bells played from a keyboard or by mechanical means.

Carol - A song. A song of praise, applied to the types of songs   sung at Christmas time.

Cartridge TV - Audio-visual equipment which has the capability of recording and/or playing back prerecorded programs through television sets.

Castanets - A pair of small pieces of hard wood, which are struck together in order to yield a percussive effect.

Castrato *(It.)* An adult male singer with female voice range.

CATV - Abbreviation for cable television.

C clef - The clef showing the position of middle C, in which are written the soprano, alto and tenor parts. *See* **THEORY - CLEFS**.

Cedez *(Fr.)* Slow down and become softer.

Celeste *(Fr.)* Bell-like keyboard instrument. An undulating beating stop, in organs. Heavenly, otherworldly, divine.

Cello *(It.)* An abbreviation of violoncello.

Cents (acoustics) - A unit of scientific and exact method of measuring intervals in music. A cent is one-hundredth of a semitone in the well-tempered scale.

Cha-cha - A Latin American dance in insistent binary rhythm.

Chaconne *(Fr.)* A Spanish dance. Also, an instrumental piece consisting of a series of variations above a ground bass.

Chalumeau *(Fr.)* The low register in clarinets.

Chamber music - Most frequently applied to concerted compositions of instrumental music in the form of string quartets or quintets. Vocal or instrumental pieces suitable for performance in a chamber-room, as opposed to a concert hall.

Chance music - Music which permits the performer to play various sections of a composition in any order he chooses.

Change of mode - Occurs when the major tonality changes to minor tonality, or vice versa, on the same tonal center.

Changes - Harmonic progression of a tune; the chords for whatever melody is being used. In jazz, chord progressions. *See* **JAZZ**.

Chanson *(Fr.)* Song.

Chant *(Fr.)* Melody, theme, song.

Chart - In jazz, an arrangement. Also, published ranking of records in terms of sales.

Chest register - Register used predominantly by all male singers.

Chicago style - In Jazz, a slight departure from New Orleans style, popular during the 1920's.

Chiesa *(It.)* Church.

Chimes - A percussion instrument consisting of about eighteen metal tubes suspended from a metal frame and struck with a hammer.

Chinese block - A temple block. It consists of a hollowed-out wooden block played with a drumstick.

Choir *(see chorus)* A company of singers; part of a church appropriated to singers.

Choirmaster - The leader of a choir.

Choral - Music that is sung by a choir or chorus.

Chorale - A hymn tune or sacred tune.

Chorale prelude - Generally a chorale for four voices which contains the chorale melody (Cantus Firmus), motivic material derived from the chorale melody and additional accompanying material.

Chord - Simultaneous sound of three or more tones. *See* **THEORY** - **CHORD TYPES**.

Chord changes - A series of successive chords.

Chord symbols - Symbols in letter form which are a shorthand method of indicating the chords which are to determine the harmonic structure of a piece. *See* **THEORY - JAZZ CHORD TYPES**.

Chorister - The conductor or leader of a choir or chorus.

Chorus - A body of singers; the refrain of a song; a composition for a body of singers. Also, in jazz, a musical form delineating a chord structure or progression which, in its totality, forms the basis for an improvisation.

Chromatic - See accidental.

Chromaticism - The use of chromatic intervals and of chords altered by chromatic means.

Chromatic scale *(see scale)* - A scale consisting of twelve halftones to the octave. *See* **THEORY - SCALES AND MODES.**

Church modes - Scales employed in medieval church music. *See* **THEORY - SCALES AND MODES.**

Circle of fifths - A succession of perfect fifths which, in the well-tempered system, return to the initial tone after twelve progressions.

Clarinet - A wind instrument with a beating reed.

Classical - The period between 1750 and 1820 characterized by the music of Mozart, Haydn, and early Beethoven.

Claves - A Cuban percussion instrument consisting of two round sticks of hard wood which are beaten together.

Clavichord - The predecessor of the piano widely used from the 16th through the 18th centuries. A keyboard instrument with horizontal strings struck by brass tangents.

Clavier *(Ger.)* Keyboard.

Clefs - From the Latin Clavin meaning key. A sign placed at the beginning of the staff to indicate a specific pitch. *See* **THEORY - CLEFS.**

Closed-circuit television - An integral system in which television signals are transmitted by coaxial cable or microwave link to interconnected receivers.

Close harmony - Occurs when the upper three voices are as close together as possible. Soprano and tenor are usually never more than an octave apart.

Close structure - Occurs when there is an octave or less between the soprano and tenor.

Clusters - When a passage is dominated by chords by seconds and arranged in predominantly uninverted forms so that most of the voices are a second apart, the chords are called clusters.

Coda *(It.)* End, concluding passage.

Codetta *(It.)* A short coda or extra concluding passage usually located in the interior of a composition or movement.

Col, colla, colle *(It.)* With the.

Col legno *(It.) (Ger.)* With the wood of the bow.

Coloratura *(It.)* Roulades, embellishments, or ornamental passages in vocal music. A voice description.

Combo - Short for combination; a small jazz ensemble.

Comic opera - An opera with a comic subject.

Commercial - Music or musicianship designed solely to garner money and/or fame. Also, a radio or television advertising spot.

Commissioned work - A commission is granted to a composer when he is asked to write an original concert work for payment and a guarantee of performance.

Common chord - An older term for the major triad. The term used for the pivot chord in modulation, the chord being common both to the original key and to the new key.

Common time - Time with two beats in a bar or any multiple of two beats in a bar. Common time is of two kinds: simple and compound. *See* **THEORY - NOTATION.**

Common tone - A tone found in two consecutive chords that occurs in the same relative position in each chord.

Comping - In jazz, furnishing the rhythmic/harmonic background.

Composer - One who writes music.

Composition - Music in any form for instruments or voices.

Compound meters - Meters which use triple units. *See* **THEORY - METERS.**

Compressed score - A score in which more than one part is placed on a staff.

Con *(It.) (Sp.)* With.

Concert - A performance of music.

Concert band - An instrumental group comprised of woodwinds, brasses, and percussion. Also Symphonic band.

Concert grand - A grand piano.

Concertina - The improved accordion invented by Wheatstone in 1829.

Concertino - The solo group in the Baroque concerto grosso.

Concert master - The first violinist of an orchestra.

Concerto *(It.)* A piece of several movements for one or more solo instruments with orchestra; sometimes one solo instrument with piano.

Concerto grosso *(It.)* A concertino for instruments utilizing a small group of soloists accompanied by full orchestra.

Concert pitch - The actual sound produced by an instrument as opposed to a written note in transposing instruments.

Concord - The opposite of discord. A combination of harmonious sounds.

Conduct - To direct a performance of music in a unified musical effort by means of manual and bodily motions. *See* **THEORY - CONDUCTING FRAMES.**

Conductor - The leader or director of a music group.

Conjunct degree - The nearest tone in the diatonic or chromatic scale to the given tone.

Conservatory - From the Italian, Conservatorio, a school dedicated to the teaching and learning of music.

Consonance - A relation or state of relative rest or relaxation between various tones that produces an agreeable effect.

Consonant chord - A chord containing no dissonant interval.

Con sordino *(It.)* Muted.

Consort - A 17th century English term for instrumental chamber ensembles or for music written for them.

Continuo *(It.)* In baroque music, continuous bass accompaniment.

Contrabass - Double bass.

Contractor - A union musician who hires the services of other union members for the purpose of performing.

Contralto *(It.)* Literally, a deeper alto. Often used to mean alto.

Contrapuntal - In the style of counterpoint.

Contrary motion - Occurs when two voices move in opposite directions.

Copyright registration - The placing on record in the Copyright Office claims of copyright.

Corda *(It.)* String.

Cornet - Corneta *(Sp.)* Modern brass instrument, having valves or pistons by means of which a complete chromatic scale can be produced.

Corno *(It.)* Horn, French horn.

Corps *(Fr.)* A band of musicans; the body of a musical instrument.

Counterpoint - The art of writing independent melodies against each other.

Courante *(Fr.)* An old dance; flowing, rapid, running.

Cow bells - Percussion instruments, struck with a drumstick, similar to the bells worn by cows.

CPU (Central Processing Unit) - The primary unit of a microcomputer that includes the circuits controlling the interpretation and execution of instructions.

Crab canon - See canon crancrizan.

Crab movement - The backward movement of a melody.

Crescendo *(It.)* Swelling, becoming louder.

Cross flute - A flute held across the mouth, and blown from the side.

Crossover network - In multiple loudspeaker systems, a circuit employing electrical filters of frequency discriminating paths for routing high, low, and middle frequencies to the particular speakers designed to handle them.

Cross rhythm - The simultaneous use of conflicting rhythmic patterns.

Crumhorn - Used in Europe in the 16th and 17th centuries, a slender hook-shaped wind instrument with a double reed.

Cue - A catch word or phrase. The last notes or words of other parts inserted as a guide to singers, players, or actors who have to make an entry after rests. Also, part of the circuitry of the mixing console which enables the engineer in the control room and the musicians in the studio to communicate via headphones.

Cycle (acoustics) - A complete sound wave moving to point of highest displacement through point of lowest displacement and back to point of highest displacement.

Cycle or Cyclical forms - Sonatas, symphonies and suites are examples of cycle forms, because they are made up of several complete movements and forms.

Cyclic relationships - Refers to the relationship of chords through the cycle of fifths, cycle of fourths, cycle of thirds, cycle of seconds, etc.

Dd

D - The second note in the scale of C major. Abbreviation for da, dal, or destra.

Da capo *(It.)* From the beginning.

Dal segno *(It.)* From the sign.

Damper - Moveable pieces of mechanism in a piano for checking the vibration of a string; damper pedal is the right side pedal of a piano; damper is also the mute of a horn or other brass instrument.

Dance - A rhythmic movement of the body, usually to the accompaniment of music.

D.C. *(It.)* Da capo. The head.

Decay - The amplitude characteristics at the end of a sound in electronic music.

Decay time - The time (in seconds) which it takes for a sound to decay to a level 60 decibels below its original level. It is normally known as RT60.

Deceptive cadence - A cadence in which the dominant chord does not resolve to the tonic in octave position.

Decibel (acoustics) - Scientific unit for measuring loudness or intensity of sound.

Decrescendo *(It.)* Becoming softer.

Degrees - The tones of a scale. The *degrees* are numbered from one to seven: 1. Do, Tonic 2. Re, Supertonic 3. Mi, Mediant 4. Fa, Subdominant 5. Sol, Dominant 6. La, Submediant, 7. Ti, Leading tone.

Demo - Abbreviation for demonstration, usually referring to tapes or records used for marketing or testing.

Dependent chord - A dissonant chord requiring resolution to a consonant chord.

Derivative work - A music arrangement based on a previously written composition.

Descant *(Lat.)* An independent melody which is composed to accompany another melody.

Descriptive music - See program music.

Desk - An orchestral music-stand shared by two players. Also, see console.

Detache *(Fr.)* Alternate up and down bows in string bowing.

Deux *(Fr.)* Two.

Development - The evolution or elaboration of a theme, melodically, harmonically, or rhythmically.

Diabolus in Musica *(It.)* Another name for the tritone which was considered in the 15th and 16th centuries, the "most dangerous" interval.

Diatonic - An order of tones expressed by the white keys of the piano; concerning scales with progressing *degrees* of different names.

Diatonic chord - A chord whose tones conform to a diatonic scale.

Dictation - The recognition and identification of specific elements of music aurally without reference to the score. It is analysis by ear rather than by eye.

Digital - A keyboard key. Also, the binary code: the 01011001 - style numeric language on which all computers are based.

Digital computer - An arithmetical calculating machine that processes data and solves problems in symbolic or numerical form.

Diminished - Made less. Smaller than minor or perfect. *See* **THEORY - CHORD TYPES, INTERVALS.**

Diminished seventh chord - A chord comprised of a diminished triad and diminished seventh interval above the root. *See* **THEORY - CHORD TYPES.**

Diminished triad - A chord comprised of a minor third and a diminished fifth. *See* **THEORY - CHORD TYPES.**

Diminuendo *(It.)* Becoming softer.

Diminution - Refers to the shortening of note values in a melodic line.

Dirge - A funeral hymn.

Discord - Dissonance.

Disk storage - A computer network section where information is stored on disk files.

Dissonance - A relation or state of tension between various tones.

Dissonant chord - A chord containing one or more dissonant intervals.

Divertimento *(It.)* An instrumental work of short movements.

Divisi *(It.)* Indicating several parts where there is normally only one.

Dixieland - A syncopated jazz style thought to have started in New Orleans c. 1915, utilizing collective improvisation and dotted rhythms. Typical instrumentation included drums, piano, banjo, clarinet, cornet or trumpet, and sometimes trombone and tuba.

Do *(It.)* The syllable applied to the tonal center of a scale in singing. In the "fixed" Do system, Do is always C. The French use UT instead of Do in instrumental music. *See* **degrees**.

Dodecaphonic music - A method of composition involving twelve tones which are related only with one another. Used synonomously with the terms twelve-tone music and serial music.

Dolce *(It.)* Smooth, sweet, gently, A fairly soft foundation stop in organs.

Doloroso *(It.)* Lamenting, grieving.

Dominant - Sol, referring to the fifth degree of a scale. *See* **degrees**.

Dominant cadence - The cadence progression from dominant to tonic. *See* **cadence**.

Dorian mode - Similar to the natural minor except that its sixth is raised. *See* **THEORY - SCALES AND MODES**.

Dot - Used after a note to indicate augmentation of its value by one-half; above a note to indicate staccato. *See* **THEORY - NOTATION**.

Double-bar - Two vertical lines drawn through the staff at the end of a section, movement or piece.

Double bass - The largest and deepest-toned instrument played with a bow.

Double concerto - Concerto for two instruments and orchestra.

Double counterpoint - *See* **invertible counterpoint.**

Double flat - The symbol (♭♭) placed before the head of a note lowers its pitch two half-steps.

Double reed - The vibrating reed of instruments of the oboe class.

Double sharp - The notation (x) placed before the head of a note raises its pitch two half-steps.

Double-stop - The execution of two simultaneous notes on the violin or other string instrument.

Down-beat - The interval pulse of a measure of music. The primary beat.

Down bow sign - A sign used in string music indicating that the bow is to be drawn down. *See* **THEORY - SIGNS.**

Doxology - A hymn or song of praise.

Dramatic music - Music composed to accompany a drama; program music.

Drift - In electronic music, a change brought about by some equipment malfunction, usually oscillator frequency.

D.S. *(It.)* Dal segno.

Dub-down - In electronic music composition, a process in which two or more channels of recorded audio material are combined into a single channel by means of a mixer.

Due *(It.)* Two.

Duet, duo *(Fr.)* A composition for two voices or instruments or for two performers upon one instrument.

Duet *(Fr.)* A composition composed or arranged for two performers.

Dumb piano - A small keyboard, for silent finger practice, without strings and hammers.

Dump, dumpe - In 4/4 meter, an old dance in slow time with an unusual rhythm. Also, (in computers) off-load. Usually applied when a program is dumped, or off-loaded to a storage medium such as disk or cassette.

Duo *(It.)* Duet.

Duple meter - Regular grouping to time units by two. *See* **THEORY - METERS**.

Dur *(Ger.)* Major, major key.

Duration - A relative length of a tone or rest.

Dynamic indications - Directions for nuances of loud and soft, such as crescendi, diminuendi and sforzandi. These are not terms relative to elements of harmonic rhythm, but are used to confirm the natural rhythmic feeling already present in music. *See* **THEORY - TEMPO AND EXPRESSION TERMS**.

Dynamics - Varying and contrasting degrees of intensity or loudness. *See* **THEORY - SIGNS**.

Ee

E *(It.)* And, is. The third note of the scale of C major.

Ear training - A field of instruction designed to teach students to recognize and write down musical sounds and rhythms.

Ecclesiastical modes - Octave scales used in medieval church music.

Echapee - A non-harmonic tone which is usually approached from a harmonic tone one scale step below, and then leaps downward to a harmonic tone. *See* **THEORY - NONHARMONIC TONES.**

Echo chamber - An enclosed space that has a high reverberation capacity and resonance factor.

Ecossaise *(Fr.)* Scottish, in Scottish style.

Educational music - Music composed and arranged for school use and by private music teachers.

Eighth-note (quaver) - A unit of music notation which receives one-half the time value of a quarter note. *See* **THEORY - NOTATION.**

Eighth-rest - The rest indicating silence for one-half the time value of a quarter note. *See* **THEORY - NOTATION.**

Einfach *(Ger.)* Plain, simple; single.

Einsatz *(Ger.)* An entrance, an attack.

Electric bass - A bass, consisting of the usual 4 strings (E,A,D,G) which is shaped like a large guitar and is amplified electronically.

Electronic instruments - Instruments in which the tone is produced, modified, or amplified by electronic circuits.

Electronic music - Music which is produced on electronic instruments. The term also includes electric instruments that simulate the sound of the organ, guitar, or other conventional instruments. It also refers to a kind of music which originated in the Studio for Electronic Music of the West German Radio.

Electronic music studio - A place where electronic music is created which includes tape recorders, sound modifiers, and sound sources.

Elegy - A composition of a mournful and commemorative character.

Eleventh - An interval comprised of an octave and a fourth.

Embellishment - Same as coloratura, ornamentation, etc.

Embouchure *(Fr.)* The mouthpiece of a wind instrument. The position and management of the mouth and lips of the player.

Emu *(Fr.)* With feeling.

Encore *(Fr.)* Once more, again, still.

English horn - An instrument of the oboe family which transposes a fifth below the written note.

Enharmonic - The same pitch given two different letter names in the equal tempered scale.

Ensemble *(Fr.)* Together, group of performers.

Entr'acte *(Fr.)* Music played between the acts.

Envelope - The amplitude of a signal: attack, initial decay, sustain, and final decay. Envelope generators can control both the amount of duration of each of these characteristics.

Epilogue - A concluding piece, or part.

Episode - A middle or intermediate section of a composition. A digression from the principal theme in the fugue.

Equalizer - Electronic components which alter the response of a transmission circuit in a specified way.

Equal temperament (acoustics) - A system of tuning whereby the octave is divided into twelve equal semitones.

Equivocal chord - A dissonant chord of uncertain resolution.

Escape tone - A nonharmonic tone derived step-wise leaping to a harmonic tone. *See* **THEORY - NONHARMONIC TONES.**

Espressivo *(It.)* With feeling, with expression.

Essential tones - Tones which form the accepted harmonic elements of any period of writing.

Ethnomusicology - Presently the accepted term for what was previously known as comparative musicology. The latter name derives from the fact that the approach to the study of music of various peoples was in the earlier days of the field mainly comparative. Each musical culture is now investigated in terms of its own society and geographical area.

Ethos *(Gr.)* Greek scales.

Etouffe *(Fr.)* Damped, muted, choked, stifled.

Etude *(Fr.)* A study or exercise with some particular technical problem stressed.

Etwas *(Ger.)* Somewhat.

Euphonium - Similar to the baritone horn in modern instruments. An instrument invented by Chladni in 1790, consisting of graduated glass tubes connected with steel rods.

Euphonium, double - A euphonium with two bells, either of which may be activated by a switch.

Eurhythmics - A system of music training in which students are taught to represent complex rhythmic movement with their entire bodies, introduced by Jaques-Dalcroze in 1910.

Evaded cadence - See deceptive cadence.

Exercise - A technical study for training fingers for instrumental performance; a short study in composition or theory.

Exposition - The initial section of musical forms which contains the thematic material.

Expressionism - A modern movement in music which began in the early part of the 20th-century, in which anxious moods, characteristic of modern life, were reflected through atonally constructed melodies and unorthodox rhythms.

Expression mark - A word, phrase, or sign indicating how a composition is to be performed. *See* **THEORY - SIGNS.**

Extemporize - To improvise, to perform spontaneously.

Eye music - A term often used to describe contemporary music scores that contain graphic symbols, visual patterns, and unusual methods of notation.

Ff

F *(It.)* Abbreviation for forte. The fourth note of the scale of C major.

Fagott *(Ger.)* Bassoon.

Fake book - Any of the various books containing the basic chord progressions and melodies for many songs, an indispensable book for many musicians.

False cadence - *See* **deceptive cadence**.

Falsetto *(It.)* Like the falsetto voice; high-pitched and light in quality.

Familiar style - In Renaissance vocal polyphonic music, note-against-note texture, usually in four parts, in which each syllable is sung together by all voices.

Fandango *(Sp.)* A lively dance in triple meter.

Fanfare - A flourish of trumpets or trumpet call.

Fantasia, con *(It., Sp.)* With imagination, freely.

Fantasy - An instrumental composition in the free form.

Farandole *(Fr.)* A very rapid circle-dance in 6/8 meter.

Farce - A one-act opera of burlesque character.

F clef - Clef which locates small F on the five-line staff. The bass clef. *See* **THEORY - CLEFS**.

Feedback (also acoustic feedback) - The howling, oscillation, or regeneration of sound caused by a system's microphonic pick-up of the sound output from its own speakers.

Feminine ending - One which closes on a metrically weak beat.

Fermata *(It.)* A pause, usually indicated by the sign. *See* **THEORY - SIGNS**.

Festival - A series of performances.

FF *(It.)* Abbreviation for fortissimo.

Fiddle - A violin.

Fidelity - The measure of the degree of exactness with which sound is duplicated or reproduced.

Fifth - The fifth degree of the diatonic scale; an interval of five diatonic steps.

Figure - A small grouping of notes capable of being identified as a basis from which the phrase is created.

Figured bass - A system of musical shorthand whereby chords are indicated by figures placed below the bass line.

Figured melody - Florid, ornamented melody.

Film music - A 20th century extension of incidental or program music, intended to introduce and highlight the action of a film.

Finale *(It.)* The closing piece. The last movement in a symphony or sonata.

Final mix (mixdown) - The final blending together of all the separate elements that have been taped during a recording session resulting in a finished master tape.

Fine *(It.)* End.

Fingerboard - A long strip of hardwood fixed to the neck of a string instrument over which the strings are stretched.

Finger holes - The holes bored at different places in the side of the tubes of woodwind instruments which allows the player to produce different tones by covering or uncovering.

First-movement form - Sonata Allegro form.

Five, The Russian - The 19th-century nationalistic composers Balakirev, Borodin, Cui, Mussorgsky, and Rimsky-Korsakov.

Fixed Do - The system in which Do is always C, as opposed to the moveable Do system in which Do represents the tonic or key note.

Flamenco - A Spanish dance.

Flat - The symbol (♭) placed before the head of a note which lowers its pitch one-half tone.

Flautist - A flute player.

Flemish School - Major developers of the polyphonic style of the 15th and 16th-centuries from the Netherlands and Belgium.

Flip side - The reverse and, usually, less important side of a phonograph record.

Florid - Embellished with trills, figures, runs, grace notes, etc.

Flourish - A trumpet fanfare.

Flugelhorn (*Ger.*) Flugelhorn. A brass instrument similar to but larger than the cornet. A solo reed stop designed to imitate the tone of the flugelhorn in organs.

Flute (*Fr.*) Flute. An orchestral instrument which has a metal or wooden tube of cylindrical bore, with 14 holes closed by keys, blown through an oval orifice near the upper end.

Flute, alto - Pitched in G, a fourth below the regular flute, it is also larger.

Flute, piccolo - The smallest flute which sounds one octave above the regular flute.

Flutter-tongue - A special effect in wind playing, produced by a rapid fluttering of the tongue in or about the mouthpiece.

Flying staccato - Skipping the bow across the strings in violin music.

Folk song - A simple, unaffected song of the people.

Foreign chords or tones - Chords or tones which do not belong to a given key or chord.

Form - The organization of all elements of a composition to achieve a certain aesthetic logic.

Forte *(It.)* Loud. Also, f.

Fortissimo *(It.)* Very loud, Also, ff, fff.

Forzando *(It.)* A sharp accent. *See* **sforzando.**

Four-hand piano - Music written for 2 piano players on one instrument; one playing the treble parts (primo) and the other the bass (secondo).

Four-part writing - A harmonic concept of writing music widely used in the 18th and 19th centuries. The term implies, vertically, four factors in each chord and, horizontally, four different melodic lines.

Fourth - The fourth degree of the diatonic scale; an interval of four diatonic steps.

Fourth chords - Chords consisting of superimposed fourths, e.g., F B♭ E♭ A♭, etc.

Fox trot - A ballroom dance in duple or quadruple meter which began in the 1920's.

Free canon - A canon in which one or more of the melodic lines is altered by adding sharps, flats, or omitting notes.

Free style - In composition, a relaxation of the rules of strict counterpoint.

French harp - Mouth organ.

French horn - A brass instrument, with a tunnel-shaped opening, the shape of a spiral. It may be pitched in F or B♭ or both. When in F it sounds a fifth lower than the written note.

French sixth chord - A sixth chord which employs the use of the augmented six-four-three chordal arrangement. *See* **THEORY - SIXTH CHORDS**.

Frequency (acoustics) - The number of cycles of sound waves which occur each second in producing sound. Frequency determines pitch.

Frets - Small strips of wood, ivory or metal, placed upon the fingerboard of certain stringed instruments, to regulate the pitch of the notes produced.

Frog - The hand-held end of a string instrument bow.

Fuga *(It.,Lat.)* A fugue.

Fugato *(It.)* A passage treated in fugal style.

Fughetta *(It.)* A short fugue.

Fugue - The most mature form of imitative counterpoint.

Full chord - A chord in which some, or all, tones are doubled in the octave.

Fundamental (acoustic) - The basic or most pronounced tone which generates the overtones. The root of a chord. *See* **THEORY - OVERTONE SERIES**.

Fundamental position of triads - Occurs when the root of a triad is in the bass, fifth is in the soprano, and the third is in between. *See* **THEORY - CHORD INVERSIONS**.

Funeral march - A minor key march in slow 4/4 meter.

Fuoco, con *(It.)* Passionately, excited, with fire.

Fur *(Ger.)* For.

Fuzz bass - A loud and sustained sound used by rock groups produced by an amplified electric bass channeled through a distortion booster.

Gg

G - Fifth note of the scale of C major. Abbreviation for gauche.

Galliard - Spirited old French dance, in 3/4 meter, for 2 dancers.

Game theory - Used in various styles of avant-garde composition and in computer programming, a mathematical process based on probability and strategy that is used to analyze problems and select courses of action when confronted with an opponent who is doing likewise.

Gamme *(Fr.)* A scale. *See* **THEORY - SCALES AND MODES**.

Gate - An electronic instrument, the purpose of which is to control the amplitude of a signal.

Gauche *(Fr.)* Left, left-hand.

Gavotte *(Fr.)* A French dance usually in common time, strongly accented beginning on the third beat.

G clef - Another term for treble clef which locates g1 on the five-line staff. *See* **THEORY - CLEFS**.

Gebrauchsmusik *(Ger.)* Everyday music, useful music, functional music.

General pause *(Ger.)* A rest for an entire orchestra.

Generator - A fundamental tone, a root; a tone which produces a series of harmonics. In electronics, the sound source of all types of electronic signals except sine waves.

German sixth chord - A sixth chord that uses the augmented six-five-three chordal arrangement. *See* **THEORY - SIXTH CHORDS.**

Gesang *(Ger.)* Vocal part, voice, singing.

Gesangvoll *(Ger.)* Songlike.

Gestalt *(Ger.)* The form or shape of a composition perceived as a unified entity rather than as a collection of elements.

Gestopft *(Ger.)* Stopped.

Ghost note - On a wind instrument, a note de-emphasized in a series - that is, fingered, but barely blown.

Gig - In jazz, a job of any kind.

Gigue *(Fr.)* A very fast dance of English origin in triple meter.

Giocoso *(It.)* Humorous, jocose.

Gitarre *(Ger.)* Guitar.

Glee - In England, a secular composition for three or more unaccompanied solo voices.

Gliss - A shortened form of the technical musical term glissando. In jazz, applied chiefly to trumpet and especially trombone. *See* **THEORY - JAZZ ARTICULATION**.

Glissando *(It.)* A glide from one note to the next.

Glockenspiel *(Ger.)* Same as carillon in organs. Bells.

G.P. - General or grand pause.

Gospel jazz - Jazz based on gospel songs, sometimes using a call- and-response pattern, and characterized by foot-stomping and hand clapping.

Grace note - A note of very short duration, which in modern usage, takes some of the value of the preceding note. *See* **THEORY - SIGNS**.

Gran casa *(It.)* Bass drum.

Grande *(It.)* Broadly.

Grand opera - An opera which treats historical, mythological, or heroic subjects, produced in a large opera house, and usually in 5 acts.

Grand piano - Ranging from the small baby grand to the concert grand measuring more than nine feet in length, the grand piano is wing-shaped with strings, soundboard, and keyboard in a horizontal place parallel to the floor.

Graphic notation - Visual symbols used in place of traditional notes and rests to indicate musical ideas in electronic, multimedia, and aleatoric scores.

Great staff - A combination of treble and bass staves, used in compositions for piano, harp, organ, celesta, etc.

Gregorian chant - The liturgical chant of the Roman Catholic church; the earliest form of Christian church music, established by Pope Gregory I in the sixth century.

Grosse caisse *(Fr.)* Bass drum.

Ground bass - A basso ostinato. A continually repeated bass phrase.

Group - A series of notes of small time value, grouped together; a division or run; a method of setting out band parts in score. Also, two or more musicians who perform together. *See* **THEORY - ARTIFICIAL RHYTHMIC GROUPINGS.**

Gusto, con *(It.)* With style, with zest.

Guitar - A plucked string instrument with 6 strings and a compass of 3 octaves and a fourth.

Hh

H - The German B-natural. Heel in organ pedaling. Hand in piano music. Abbreviation for horn in French horn.

Habanera *(Sp.)* A cuban dance with distinctive rhythm.

Hairpins - Colloquial name for the signs < and > indicating crescendo and diminuendo respectively.

Half note - The second largest unit in modern music notation. The half note receives half the value of a whole note. A minim. *See* **THEORY - NOTATION.**

Half rest - A rest the duration of a half note. *See* **THEORY - NOTATION**.

Half-step - Located on the piano keyboard by progresssing up and down from any black or white key to the nearest black or white key. A semitone.

Hallelujah - An invitation to praise, used in every Christian community.

Hard bop - The modern jazz or jazz style innovated in the mid 1950's on the East Coast, which retained all of the characteristics of bop but rejected the overly relaxed quality into which it had been led by West Coast jazzmen.

Hard rock - Rock which is characterized by a driving, monotonous beat, repetitive musical phrases, and the basic chord progressions using I, IV, and V. Hard rock is mostly identified with the 1950's and '60's.

Harmonic (acoustics) - Pertaining to music theory and harmony. One of the "partial tones" generated by the prime tone or fundamental. *See* **THEORY - OVERTONE SERIES**.

Harmonica - The modern mouth harmonica is a small reed instrument, played by blowing and sucking air through a series of holes, each containing a pair of reeds.

Harmonic analysis - The study of harmony dealing with the variants of fundamental structure in harmony.

Harmonic dictation - The process of identifying the functions of a tonality when music is played.

Harmonic interval - Occurs when two tones of an interval are sounded simultaneously.

Harmonic minor scale - The harmonic minor scale differs from the natural or pure minor scale in that the seventh degree is raised one-half step. *See* **THEORY - SCALES AND MODES.**

Harmonization - The process of supplying the harmony to a given melody, or to any given part.

Harp - One of the oldest known stringed instruments, the modern harp utilizes 46 to 47 gut strings, has a range of six and one- half octaves, and is built of a 3-cornered wooden frame with a curving neck.

Harpsichord - A keyboard instrument in which the strings are plucked by quills or bits of hard leather. A predecessor to the piano.

Hastig *(Ger.)* Hurrying, with haste; abruptly, suddenly.

Hawaiian guitar - A guitar which is placed horizontally and played, not with the fingers, but with a small metal bar called a steel. The pitches are changed by sliding the steel across all the strings making possible the sliding thirds which characterize Hawaiian music.

Head arrangement - In jazz, an arrangement made up in performance most often on a repeated form like the blues with musicians improvising riffs.

Head register - Utilized by female singers and corresponds in some respects to the usually underdeveloped "falsetto" in men.

Head-tones, head-voice - The vocal tones of the head-register.

Heldentenor *(Ger.)* A heroic tenor voice of great volume and brilliancy.

Hemiola - A rhythmic change in which three beats replace two beats.

Hertz - The unit of frequency. It is equal to one cycle per second and is named after Heinrich Hertz, the German physicist who discovered radio waves. Abbreviated as Hz.

Heterophony - The duplication of a melody at any interval. A characteristic of primitive music.

Hexachord - A group of six diatonic tones with a semi-tone interval in the middle.

Hidden fifth - Similar motion of voices to an open fifth in a chord progression.

Hidden octave - Similar motion of outer voices to an octave in a chord progression.

High fidelity - Recording breakthrough in the mid-1940's which achieved more brilliance, sonority, and clarity than that which came before. Abbreviated as hi-fi.

Hillbilly music - Music cultivated in America by residents of the hill country, primarily of Kentucky, Missouri, and the Appalachian mountains.

Hold - A pause or fermata. *See* **THEORY - SIGNS**.

Homage - A 20th-century composition dedicated to the name and style of a composer.

Homophony - In modern music, a style of melody supported by chords, in contrast to polyphony, which is melody supported by other melodies or parts or voices.

Hook - The curved line attached to the stem of a note. Also, in commercial music, a musical phrase, vocal or instrumental, which is repeated a number of times in a song to literally "hook" the listener. It is often synonymous with riff.

Honky-tonk - A style of ragtime piano playing, loud, gaudy, and tinny, which was performed in gin mills, houses of prostitution, and dance halls in New Orleans in the early part of the twentieth century.

Horn *(Ger.)* French horn, sometimes saxhorn. A general term in musical jargon for the brass and/or wind section of a band or orchestra. Also, the treble or high frequency portion of a PA speaker or system. The horns work in conjunction with mid-range and bass bins to give high-quality response over the entire audio range.

Hosanna *(Lat.)* Part of the Sanctus in the Mass.

Humoresque *(Fr.)* A piano piece of light, whimsical style.

Hybrid synthesizer - A synthesizer that is a combination of analog sound generating elements with digital control.

Hymn - A religious or sacred song.

Hyper *(Ger.)* Above.

Hypo *(Ger.)* Below.

Hz - Abbreviation for hertz.

Ii

I *(It.)* The. Abbreviation for primo.

Ictus - A separation mark used in Gregorian chant to stress important notes.

Idiomatic style - Writing of music appropriate for the instrument or voice.

Imitation - Repetition of a theme, motive or phrase introduced by one part, the antecedent, in another part, the consequent. An essential element of contrapuntal style.

Imperfect authentic cadence - An authentic cadence which has the third or fifth in the soprano of the tonic triad.

Imperfect plagal cadence - A plagal cadence in which the soprano note is changed in the progression IV-I.

Impresario *(It.)* An agent or manager of a concert or opera organization.

Impressionism - A term used to describe French composition of the early 20th century.

Impromptu *(Fr.)* A piece of an extemporaneous character.

Improvisation (Extemporization) - The art of musical performance without aid of memorization or notation.

Improvise - To create spontaneously.

Incidental - A tone or grace note not related to a chord.

Incidental music - Music written to go with a play or drama.

Incomplete cadence - Occurs when some tone other than the key-note is in the soprano of the tonic chord.

Indeterminacy - A type of music in the 1950's, in which certain elements are left undecided by the composer.

Inharmonic tones - Tones which do not fit in the chord structure. *See* **THEORY - NONHARMONIC TONES.**

Inner parts - The alto and tenor voices. Parts in the harmonic structure lying between the highest and lowest.

Instrument - Any mechanical contrivance for the production of sound.

Instruments - Name for all devices that produce musical sounds including stringed instruments, wind instruments, percussion instruments, and electrophones in which the acoustical vibrations are produced by electrical devices.

Intensity - A relative feeling of soft to loud.

Interlude - A passage connecting the main sections of a composition.

Intermezzo - Incidental music; a short movement interpolated between the main sections of a work.

Interval - The pitch relation or distance between two tones. Interval types are: Major, minor, perfect, augmented, and diminished. See **THEORY - INTERVALS.**

Intonation - Formerly, the production of a tone. In modern usage intonation denotes the singing or playing in tune.

Intrada *(It.)* A short prelude or introduction.

Introduction - A phrase or division preparatory to a composition or major section of a composition.

Introit - An antiphon sung while the priest proceeds to the altar to celebrate the Mass. In the Anglican church, a short anthem or hymn sung as the minister approaches the communion table.

Invention - A short piece in free contrapuntal style.

Inversion - A change of an octave in the pitch of one or more notes in an interval or chord; such chords where the bass tone is other than the root. The first inversion of a triad appears with the third in the bass and the second inversion with the fifth, etc. *See* **THEORY - CHORD INVERSIONS.**

Invertible counterpoint - Counterpoint in which two or more parts change places, e.g., the highest part becomes the bass.

Ionian mode - Same as the major mode. *See* **THEORY - SCALES AND MODES**.

Irregular meters - Meters which deviate from the normal bipartite and tripartite metrical schemes. *See* **THEORY - METERS**.

Isometric - Polyphonic music in which all the parts move at the same time in the same rhythmic values forming a succession of chords.

Istesso tempo, l' *(It.)* At the same tempo.

Italian sixth chord - An augmented sixth chord. *See* **THEORY - SIXTH CHORDS**.

Jj

Jack - The quill or hopper which strikes the strings of a harpsichord; the upright lever in piano action. In electronics, the receptacle for a plug connector leading to the input or output circuit of a tape recorder or other piece of equipment.

Jam, jam session - In jazz, an instrumental and or/vocal improvisation.

Janizary music - Military percussion music.

Jarabe *(Sp.)* Mexican dance with Spanish roots.

Jazz - A significant musical art form which has been created and developed almost solely in America and is characterized by a great degree of skillful improvisation, distinct rhythmic punctuation,and an original approach to instrumentation and orchestration.*See* **THEORY - SIGNS, JAZZ CHORD TYPES, JAZZ ARTICULATION**.

Jazz-rock - A merger of jazz and rock termed fusion, maturing in the 1960'and '70's, which featured the heavy beat of rock with electric amplification, along with the sophisticated improvisations of jazz.

Jete *(Fr.)* Striking the bow on the string so that it rebounds several times on the down-bow.

Jeune France - French composers Oliver Messiaen, Daniel Lesur, Andre Jolivet, and Yves Baudrier who banded together in 1936 to devote themselves to new music free from revolutionary and academic formulas.

Jig - A country dance in triple or compound meter.

Jingle - A radio or television ad spot used to promote a particular product usually consisting of musical material in addition to a spoken message.

Joint publishing - Two publishers share in the ownership of one copyright.

Jota *(Sp.)* A Spanish national dance.

Jubiloso *(It.)* Jubilant, exulting.

Just intonation - The correct sounding of intervals in singing or playing.

Juxtaposition of keys - A change of key without any modulatory process whatever.

Kk

K - Abbreviation for 1,000. 1k ohms = 1,000 ohms, 10k ohms = 10,000 ohms. Read as "kilo," 1kHz = "one kilo-hertz" and 1k ohm = "one kilohm."

Kanon *(Ger.)* Canon.

Kettledrum - An orchestral drum consisting of a hollow brass or copper shell, over the top of which a head of vellum or plastic is stretched.

Key - A scale, the key being the first (tonic) note of the scale. The beginning key in a piece of music. The ultimate key or ending key in comparison to other keys used in a composition. A lever opening, or closing a hole in wind instruments. The lever that is moved to make the piano action strike the strings. *See* **THEORY - KEY SIGNATURES.**

Keyboard - The whole series of levers for producing tone in a piano, harpsichord, organ, or other like-instruments.

Key click - Sometimes found in avant-garde compositions, indicated by the sign (+), a sound produced when a player strikes a key on his instrument, resulting in a hard metallic click.

Keynote - The first note of a key or scale.

Key relationship - Keys of nearest relationship to a given key are those having one sharp (or flat) more or less in the signature.

Key signature - A convenient grouping of accidentals used in a piece. *See* **THEORY - KEY SIGNATURES**.

Kit - A small pocket-violin formerly used by dancing masters.

Klangvoll *(Ger.)* Resounding, ringing.

Klavier *(Ger.)* Piano.

Klavierstuck *(Ger.)* A short piano piece or composition.

Klingen lassen *(Ger.)* Let sound.

Konzert *(Ger.)* Concert, concerto.

Kyrie eleison *(Lat.)* The first movement in a Mass.

Ll

L - Abbreviation for left. In German, hand; *see* **linke.**

Lacrimoso *(It.)* Tearful, mournful.

Laissez *(Fr.)* Let, depart, leave, leave alone.

Lament - Irish and Scottish music for the bagpipes used at funeral rites. A composition commemorating the death of a distinguished person.

Lamentoso *(It.)* Lamenting, mournful.

Lancio, con *(It.)* Flinging, with verve.

Langsam *(Ger.)* Slow.

Largamente *(It.)* Broadly.

Largando *(It.)* Slowing down, becoming broader.

Larghetto *(It.)* A slow tempo, not quite as slow as largo.

Largo *(It.)* Slow, sustained, solemn; slower than lento but not as slow as grave.

Larynx - The organ of the voice, by which we produce vocal sound, situated at the top of the wind pipe.

Lead - A cue; the giving-out of a theme by one part; the first part in jazz.

Leader - A director or conductor.

Leading-tone - The seventh degree of the scale. *See* **degrees**.

Lead sheet - A song as written down in its simplest form, melody line, chord symbols, and lyrics.

Leap - A skip; any interval larger than a second.

Lebendig *(Ger.)* Lively.

Lebhaft (Ger.) Animated, lively.

Ledger line - A short line used as an extension above and below the regular five-line staff.

Legando *(It.)* Binding.

Legato *(It.)* Even, without any break between notes, smooth.

Leggiero *(It.)* Light, delicate.

Legno, col *(It.)* Played with the wood (stick) of the bow by bouncing it against the strings.

Leicht *(Ger.,Fr.)* Light.

Leise *(Ger.)* Soft.

Leisure music - Music performed by amateurs for fun and enjoyment.

Leitmotiv *(Ger.)* Leading motive; a compositional device whereby a motive is identified with a specific character, event, etc.

Leno *(It.)* Weak, faint, feeble.

Lento *(It.,Sp.)* A slow tempo.

Lesto *(It.)* A slow tempo, usually between adagio and andante.

L.H. *(Ger.)* Abbreviation for left hand.

Level - The amplitude, or strength, of a signal. Usually expressed in dB, related to a reference level.

Liberta *(It.)* Liberty, freedom.

Libretto *(It.)* The words of an opera or oratorio in book form.

Lieblich *(Ger.)* Sweet, lovely, melodious.

Lied *(Ger.)* A song, a ballad.

Liederkranz *(Ger.)* A singing society; a song cycle.

Lieto *(It.)* Joyful, gay.

Ligature - Tones of longer duration falling upon time units which are normally weak in the scheme of metric accentuation. The predecessor of the tie used in neumatic notation. Also, a metal device used to secure a reed to the mouthpiece of a woodwind instrument.

Light opera - An operetta.

Linear counterpoint - A type of modern contrapuntal writing in which individual lines are the main considerations in the ensemble.

Linke hand *(Ger.)* Left hand.

Liscio *(It.)* Even, smooth, regular.

L'istesso tempo *(It.)* In the same tempo as the previous section.

Liturgical drama - Medieval plays during the 12th and 13th-centuries which represented Biblical stories in Latin.

Liturgy - The total service of the Christian church.

Loco *(It.)* Return to normal position.

Longitudinal wave (acoustics) - Vibrating particles moving to and fro in the same direction as the wave is traveling.

Loudness - Sound level as detected by the average human ear. The ear is more sensitive to "middle" frequencies than to low or high extremes, especially at low levels. *See* **volume.**

Loud pedal - The pianoforte pedal which lifts the dampers, the right pedal.

Lourd *(Fr.)* Strong, weighty.

Loure *(Fr.)* Like a bagpipe drone, sounding continuously; a legato but with emphasis on each note in bowing.

Luftig *(Ger.)* Light, airy.

Luftpause *(Ger.)* Pause for breath.

Lunga, lungo *(It.)* Sustained, long.

Lustig *(Ger.)* Cheerful, merry.

Lydian mode - The same as the major except that its fourth degree is raised one semitone. *See* **THEORY - SCALES AND MODES.**

Lyre - One of the most ancient of stringed instruments; a kind of harp.

Lyric - Poetry or blank verse intended to be set to music.

Lyrics - The text of a popular song or musical.

Mm

M - Abbreviation for mano or main, meaning hand, manual, metronome, etc. Also, abbreviation for 1,000,000. 1M ohms = 1,000,000 ohms; read as "meg" or "mega;" 1M ohm = "one megohm" and 1 MHz = "one megahertz."

Ma *(It.)* But.

Machine heads - Geared mechanisms on the headstock of a guitar around which the strings are wound; they are used for tuning.

Macrotonal scale - A scale composed of intervals larger than whole tones.

Madrigal - A vocal setting of a short lyric poem in three to six contrapuntal parts; usually for unaccompanied chorus.

Maggiore *(It.)* Major.

Main *(Fr.)* Hand.

Mainstream - An intermediate position between the traditionalists and the modernists.

Majeur *(Fr.)* Major.

Major-minor system - The acknowledged superior authority of major and minor modes over a period of more than three hundred years.

Major mode - Derived from a major scale which has one full or two half-steps between each degree, except between the third and fourth degree and the seventh and octave which have a half-step.

Major triad - A major triad contains a major third and a perfect fifth.

Malaguena *(Sp.)* A type of Spanish folk music in the provinces of Malaga and Murcis.

Mambo - A West Indian dance similar to the rhumba and cha-cha.

Mancando *(It.)* Decreasing; dying away.

Mandolin - A small stringed instrument generally almond-shaped.

Mano *(It.)* Hand.

Manual - An organ keyboard.

Maracas - Usually in pairs, Latin American rattle-like instruments, played by shaking.

Marcato *(It.)* Stressed, accented.

March - A composition with strongly marked rhythm, suitable for accompanying troops in walking. Generally written in 2/4 or 6/8 meter.

Marcia *(It.)* March.

Mariachi *(Sp.)* A folk singer; a Mexican instrumental ensemble.

Marimba - A musical instrument made of a series of graduated pieces of hard wood, which are struck with hammers or mallets.

Marks of expression - Words or signs used in music to regulate the degrees of accent, time, or tone required to produce the artistic effect of a composition. *See* **THEORY - TEMPO AND EXPRESSION TERMS.**

Marque *(Fr.)* Accented, marked, emphasized.

Martele *(Fr.)* Heavy, detached up-and-down strokes, played by releasing each bow stroke suddenly and using the point of the bow; in piano playing, a forceful, detached effect, created by releasing the keys suddenly.

Marziale *(It.)* Military, martial.

Masculine ending - Occurs when the final cadence falls on an accented beat; the bar line being placed just before V in the half cadence and before II in the authentic cadence.

Masque - A musical drama popular in the 16th and 17th-centuries.

Mass, Missa *(Lat.)* **Messa** *(It.)* **Messe** *(Fr.,Ger.)* In the Roman Catholic Church, the celebration of the Eucharist of Last Supper. Also celebrated in some High Anglican churches. Portions of the Mass usually set to music are the Kyrie, the Gloria, the Credo, the Sanctus, and the Agnus Dei.

Massig *(Ger.)* Moderately, a moderate tempo.

Master tape - The final multi-track recording of the two-track stereo 1/4 inch tape which carries the final mixdown from the multi-track tape and from which the master record is cut.

Mazurka *(It.)* A Polish national dance in triple meter.

Meantone tuning (acoustics) - Prior to the middle of the 19th-century in England, a compromise tuning which had a widespread vogue was the meantone tuning.

Measure - The space between two bar lines.

Medesimo *(It.)* The same.

Mediant - Referring to the third degree of the scale. *See* **degrees**.

Medieval period - The art period between 600 and 1450.

Medley - A mixture; a series of different tunes, played without interruption, usually in the same tempo.

Megaphone - A large speaking-trumpet.

Melange *(Fr.)* A medley, potpourri.

Melisma - An expressive, one-syllable, vocal passage.

Mellophone - A type of brass instrument shaped similarly to the French horn, with piston valves, a compass of two and one-half octaves, usually pitched in F.

Mellophonium - Developed by Stan Kenton and utilized mainly in jazz, the mellophonium looks like a French horn with a straight bell and is functional as a sectional or solo instrument.

Melodic dictation - The process of reproducing in musical notation a melody which has been played or sung.

Melody - An organized succession of three or more tones.

Meno *(It.)* Less.

Mensural music - Polyphonic music in which each note has a strictly determined value.

Mensurable notation - Notes invented in the 12th-century to express exact time values; more commonly "mensural notation."

Menuet *(Fr.)* A minuet; a slow dance in 3/4 meter.

Messa di voce *(It.)* A gradual swelling and subsiding on a single tone in singing or playing.

Meter - The basic scheme of note values and accents which remain unaltered throughout a composition or section thereof. *See* **THEORY - METERS.**

Metric accent - An accent which undulates between accented and unaccented beats.

Metronome - An apparatus to indicate the exact tempo of a piece of music. Invented by John Maelzel in 1815, the metronome is a device in which a weighted rod, projected upward, swings from side to side in regular time, to mark the beats of a measure. Modern metronomes are electric or of solid state.

Metronomic marks - Marks on a composition score which indicate the speed at which the composition is to be performed, e.g., a quarter note = 90 indicates a speed of 90 quarter notes or the equivalent per minute.

Mezzo, mezza *(It.)* Medium, half.

Mezzo soprano - A voice lower in range than a soprano and higher than a contralto.

Mi - Referring to the third degree of the scale. A syllable used for the third note of the scale in singing, etc. *See* **Degrees**.

Microprocessor - The control section of an integrated circuit chip. A small computer which is used in sophisticated digital outboard equipment and units such as sequencers and drum machines; also in automated or computer mixing desks.

Microtone - An interval smaller than a semitone.

Microtone scales - Scales consisting of more than twelve semitones to the octave. These scales may involve the use of quarter tones, sixth tones, eighth tones, and even smaller divisions of the octave.

Middle "c" - The "c" near the middle of the keyboard. It is located on the first ledger line above the bass staff and the first ledger line below the treble staff. *See* **THEORY - OCTAVE REGISTERS.**

MIDI (Musical Instrument Digital Interface) - A language that allows different types of music hardware (drum machines, sequencers, synthesizers, computers) to communicate with each other.

Military band - A band, consisting of woodwinds, brass, and percussion, attached to a branch or division of the military service.

Miniature score - A composition score reproduced in small size for study purposes.

Minor *(Lat.)* Less, smaller.

Minor chord - A chord comprised of a minor third and perfect fifth. *See* **THEORY - CHORD TYPES.**

Minuet - An early French dance-form in slow triple meter.

MIR - Musical Information Retrieval - A computer program intended for the theoretical analysis and cataloging of existing compositions, developed at Princeton University by Lewis Lockwood and Arthur Mendel in 1964.

Mirror canon - A canon sounding the same whether singing or playing backwards or forwards.

Missa *(Lat.)* A Mass.

Misterioso *(It.)* Mysterious, secretive.

Mit *(Ger.)* With.

Mixed chorus - A chorus or vocal which combines male and female voices.

Mixed meter - Different meters which follow each other in close succession; also referred to as multi-meter.

Mixer - In recording, a device by which signals from two or more sources can be blended and fed simultaneously into a tape recorder at the proper level and balance. Also, a studio engineer, who specializes in blending together all of the separate elements that have been taped during a recording session.

Mixing - Combining incoming signals, readjusting their relative amplitudes, and sending them to other electronic instruments.

Mixolydian - The arrangement of tones found in the scale using only the white keys of the piano from G to G. *See* **THEORY - SCALES AND MODES.**

M.M. - Abbreviation for Maelzel's metronome.

Modal - In the character of a mode, either a church mode (modal melody, harmony), or a rhythmic mode (modal rhythm, notation).

Modality - The choice of tones between which the relationship of tonality exists. The use of church modes, e.g., Lydian, Dorian, Phrygian, etc., as scale resources for composition.

Mode - A specific selection and arrangement of tones forming the tonal substance of a composition. In early times, the collective name for scales. *See* Aolian, Dorian, Ionian, Lydian, Major, Minor, Mixolydian, Phrygian *in* **THEORY - SCALES AND MODES.**

Moderato *(It.)* Neither fast nor slow; a moderate tempo.

Modern music - In "serious" music, music composition as it developed at the beginning of the 20th-century; all "popular" music, including show, jazz, rock, and pop.

Modes - Forms of scales originally used by the Greeks and later adopted by medieval musicians, especially for ecclesiastical music. *See* **THEORY - SCALES AND MODES.**

Modifier - Any electronic device that changes a characteristic or characteristics of a signal. e.g., filters, reverberation units, amplifiers, modulators, etc.

Modinha - A sentimental, romantic, Brazilian song.

Modulate - To pass from one key or mode into another.

Modulation - The process of abandoning one tonality and establishing a new one. It is usually affected by a pivot chord which belongs to both the old and new tonalities. See common chord, chromatic modulation, etc.

Modulation, deceptive - Modulation which leads to an unexpected harmony and deceives the ear.

Modus lascivus - The Ionian mode, same as the major scale of C.

Moll *(Ger.)* Minor.

Molto *(It.)* Very, much.

Monaural recorder - Literally, a tape recorder intended for listening with one ear only; however, in popular usage refers to single channel recorders, as distinguished from multi-channel (stereophonic, binaural, etc.) types. More correctly, but less universally called "monophonic" recorder.

Monitor loudspeaker - A speaker used in studio control rooms to determine quality or balance. Also, speakers used by performers on stage so that they can hear themselves.

Monophonic - A single melodic line without other parts or chordal accompaniment. A recording on a single track.

Monothematic - A single-subject composition.

Monotone *(Fr.)* Monotonous, very even; a single unvaried and unaccompanied tone.

Mordent *(Ger.)* A musical ornament consisting of the alternation of the written note with the note immediately below it. *See* **THEORY - MUSICAL ORNAMENTS.**

Morendo *(It.)* Fading away.

Morris dance - A rustic dance usually performed in spring and summer time.

Mosso *(It.)* Moved, agitated.

Motet - A sacred vocal composition in contrapuntal style performed without accompaniment.

Motif *(Fr.)* A motive, or figure.

Motive - The briefest intelligible and self-contained fragment of a musical theme or subject.

Moto *(It.)* Motion, movement.

Motown - Black rhythm and blues music emanating from Detroit; also, the recording company label that features this music.

Mouthpiece - That part of a wind instrument which is put into the mouth of the perfomer to assist in generating and altering the sound.

Movement - The various complete and comparatively independent divisions which form the sonata, symphony, etc.

Movieola - A special projection device through which a composer can listen to music tracks while watching the picture through a glass window.

Multimedia, mixed media - A presentation, performance, lesson, or series of lessons that incorporates and integrates various media, such as films, slides, tapes, music, lights, and live performances.

Multiphonics - The technique (particularly on wind instruments) of obtaining two or more voices simultaneously. Obtained by control of the overtone series in such a way that one of the partials becomes prominent enough to be heard as a separate tone. A third voice can then be added by humming.

Multiple tracking, in recording - The practice of recording a musician "over" himself. This technique, also referred to as "stacking," may be repeated as many times as there are free tracks available.

Mus.B. - Bachelor of Music.

Mus.D. - Doctor of Music.

Music - From the Greek word "muse," the art and science of combining instrumental and/or vocal sounds in various combinations of melody, harmony, rhythm, and timbre so as to create original designs, architecturally and emotionally.

Musical comedy - Today even more commonly referred to as "musical" or "broadway musical," musical comedy evolved in the United States and Britain during the 20th-century from comic opera and operetta.

Musical ornaments - *See* **THEORY - MUSICAL ORNAMENTS.**

Musicology - The science of music which includes history, esthetics, theory, bibliography, lexicography, etc.

Music drama - The original term for opera.

Music Educators Journal - The official magazine of the Music Educators National Conference.

Music Educators National Conference (MENC) - A voluntary, non-profit organization representing all phases of music education in schools, colleges, universities, and teacher-education institutions.

Musique concréte *(Fr.)* Music involving the use of natural sounds and noises, e.g., the wind, a motor accelerating, or a door slamming, etc.

Mute - A small article of wood, metal, ivory or plastic on the bridge of a string instrument to dampen the sound. A pear or cup-shaped article, made of wood, plastic, or metal used to dampen the sound of brass instruments. In recording, a switch found on some recording consoles which reduces the overall monitor level by more than half.

Nn

Nach *(Ger.)* Behind, after; according to, in the manner of.

Nacht-musik *(Ger.)* Literally night music; a serenade.

Nach und nach *(Ger.)* Little by little.

Naked fifth - A harmonic fifth without an added third.

NARAS Institute - The educational arm of the National Academy of Recording Arts and Sciences.

National Academy of Recording Arts and Sciences (NARAS) - An organization composed of individuals actively engaged in the field of recording.

National Endowment for the Arts - An agency of the federal government. Its purpose is to promote the arts, develop public support for them, and administer grants to be used for artistic endeavors.

Nationalism - Music based on nationalistic elements.

Natural - The natural sign (♮) indicates that, after a sharp or flat, the original basic tone is to be restored.

Natural harmonic - A harmonic produced on the open string of a stringed instrument. *See* **THEORY - SIGNS**.

Natural horn - The predecessor to the modern French horn, one without valves or keys, called the Waldhorn.

Neapolitan major and minor scales - *See* **THEORY - SCALES AND MODES**.

Neapolitan sixth chord - The triad on the lowered supertonic, in c minor, D-flat, F, A-flat, traditionally used in first inversion. *See* **THEORY - SIXTH CHORDS**.

Neck - That part of the instruments of the violin and guitar family which lies between the peg box and the belly.

Neighboring tone - The upper or lower second of a harmonic tone which returns to the original tone. *See* **THEORY - NONHARMONIC TONES**.

Neoclassiciam - A 20th-century movement in which composers have included features of 17th and 18th-century music.

Neoromanticism - A term to describe the mellowing trend in contemporary composition.

Neume - A nod or a sign; signs or accents used to indicate the rise and fall of the voice.

Neumes - The factors of Middle Age notation.

New music - A term used to describe the experimental trends in 20th-century composition beginning about 1910.

New Orleans style - In jazz, the original style that emerged c.1890 in Storyville, the red light district of New Orleans.

Ninth - The interval of an octave and a second. *See* **THEORY - INTERVALS.**

Nocturne *(Fr.)* A piece of a romantic character. A night piece.

Node (acoustics) - On a vibrating string, the point of least displacement.

Noel *(Fr.)* A Christmas song; derived from nouvelles, meaning "tidings."

Nonet - A piece for nine performers.

Nonharmonic tones - Any tones which do not belong to the underlying harmony. *See* **THEORY - NONHARMONIC TONES.**

Notation - The science of expressing music in writing. *See* **THEORY - NOTATION.**

Note - A symbol used to express the pitch and duration of musical tones. *See* **THEORY - NOTATION**.

Notehead - The head or principal part of a note as distinguished from its stem and hook, or flag.

Nuance *(Fr.)* Variety of intonation, shading.

Number - A single piece on a program; an opus number, a portion of a larger work, e.g., an aria, interlude, song, etc; a subdivision of an oratorio or opera.

Oo

O *(It.,Sp.)* **Or** *(Port.)* The. In medieval music, triple or perfect time. Placed over a note in string music it indicates an open string or harmonic; for brass instruments, an unstopped, unmuted note; for woodwind instruments, a harmonic should be played by overblowing; in chordgrid guitar-diagrams, an open string.

Obbligato *(It.)* An essential part in baroque music. An optional part in some 19th-century music. An accompanying melody played by a different instrument, less prominent and in a secondary role to that of the main melody.

Oblique motion - One voice remaining on the same pitch while the other moves up or down.

Oboe *(Ger.,It.)* A double-reed instrument, with 9 to 14 keys, mounted on a conical wooden tube, having a compass of two and one-half octaves.

Ocarina *(It.)* A bird-shaped wind instrument with a whistle mouthpiece and finger holes.

Octave - An interval consisting of eight diatonic tones. The eighth tone of the diatonic scale. *See* **THEORY - INTERVALS**.

Octave key - A key on wind instruments that raises the sound of other keys by one octave.

Octave marks, 8va, 8va basso - When 8va is placed over a note, the note is to be played an octave higher. A line extending from the 8va shows that all notes under the line are to be played an octave higher. 8va basso, placed under a note or notes, transposes an octave downward. *See* **THEORY - OCTAVE REGISTERS.**

Octet - A composition for eight performers.

Ode - A musical work of praise; a chorus in ancient Greek plays.

Offertory - A hymn, prayer, anthem or instrumental piece sung or played during the celebration of Holy Communion or performed during the offering.

Open chord - A chord built in perfect fourths or perfect fifths which has an open or hollow sound.

Open fifth, open octave - A fifth or triad without the third.

Open harmony - See open structure.

Open notes - Of string instruments, the notes of the open strings. Of wind instruments, the series of natural harmonics which can be produced by the lips without the assistance of a slide, key or piston.

Open structure - A spacing of the notes in a chord where there is more than an octave between the soprano and tenor.

Opera *(It.)* The musical form of drama, set to music for voices and instruments and produced with scenic effects.

Opera ballet - Popular during the 17th and 18th-centuries, a French stage work combining opera and ballet in three to four acts.

Opera bouffe *(Fr.)* Comic opera, often satirical.

Opera comique *(Fr.)* French opera, not necessarily comic, with spoken dialogue instead of recitative.

Opera seria *(It.)* Serious, tragic, heroic, or grand opera.

Operetta *(It.)* A little opera.

Opus *(Lat.)* Work; used by composers to number the order in which their works are written.

Oratorio *(It.)* A composition consisting of solos and concerted pieces for voices, the theme of which is taken from the Bible or from sacred history.

Orchestra - A group of musicians who perform on a collection of instruments in which strings are prominent, thereby distinguishing it from a band or wind ensemble.

Orchestration - The art/science of combining the instruments utilized in the symphony orchestra. The art of scoring music for an orchestra.

Ordinary - The fixed portion of all Roman Catholic services.

Organ - A keyboard musical wind instrument containing various wooden or metallic pipes made to sound by means of compressed air from bellows, and played by means of keys. The modern organ's source of energy is electronic.

Organum *(Lat.)* Church music of the early Christian era characterized by two parts moving in parallel fourths and fifths.

Oriental scale - A synthetic scale consisting of seven notes with intervals, half-step, step and a half, half-step, half-step, step and a half, and half-step. *See* **THEORY - SCALES AND MODES**.

Ornament - An embellishment.

Ornamentation - A spontaneous act on the part of the interpreter who, in performing a written or traditional melody, enlivens it, expands it, or varies it through his technique of improvisation. A compositional technique. The use of ornaments (trills, turns, etc.) in a melody. *See* **THEORY - MUSICAL ORNAMENTS**.

Oscillator - A device that produces sine wave signals at frequencies between 20 and 20,000 Hz, normally for purposes of sound synthesis or testing.

Oscilloscope - An instrument that reproduces a graphical representation of signals as voltages with respect to time on a cathode ray tube. Used to determine amplitude frequency, and wave form characteristics.

Ossia *(It.)* Or, or else, an alternative version.

Ostinato *(It.)* A steady bass accompaniment, repeated over and over.

Ottava *(It.)* Usually meaning an octave higher or lower in pitch, octave. 8va, 8a, 8.

Ottava alto *(It.)* One octave higher.

Ottava bassa *(It.)* One octave lower.

Outer voices - The highest and lowest voices.

Overblowing (acoustics) - The phenomenon which occurs when a wind instrument is blown harder or with a different lip and tongue setting resulting in the harmonic partials becoming so prominent as to dominate the fundamental.

Overdubbing - Adding new sound to previously recorded material on a spare track, or tracks, of multitrack tape.

Overtones (acoustics) - The tones generated above a fundamental tone by secondary vibrations of the main wave.

Overtone series - Tones which are related to the first (fundamental) tone sounded. A series of higher tones, or upper partials, which, when the first or fundamental is sounded, make up a complex musical tone. *See* **THEORY - OVERTONE SERIES.**

Pp

P *(It.)* Abbreviation for piano, meaning soft; also, abbreviation for pedal and prime.

Panchromatic - Inclusive of all chromatic tones. Usually used to refer to cluster chord in which all or most of the twelve (traditional) pitches occur.

Panchromatic chord - A group of notes sounded simultaneously that contain most or all of the twelve pitches in the chromatic scale.

Panning - In electronic music composition, a technique in which the sound image moves from one loudspeaker to another.

Panpipes - Invented by the god Pan, a set of reeds of different sizes.

Pantomine - An entertainment in which not a word is spoken or sung, but the sentiments are expressed by gesticulation accompanied by music.

Parallel chords - The successsive sounding of a fixed chordal combination, consonant, or dissonant, through various degrees of the scale.

Parallel fifths - Two voices moving in parallel motion from one perfect fifth to another perfect fifth.

Parallel harmony - Used extensively in impressionistic music, jazz, and rock; it involves the successive movement of a chord structure to different pitch levels.

Parallel keys - The major and minor founded on the same key note.

Parallel motion - Two or more melodic lines which move at the same interval spacing from one position to the next.

Parallel octaves - Two voices moving in parallel motion from one perfect octave to another perfect octave.

Parlando *(It.)* A style approximating speech, usually in rapid tempo, in vocal music; in a declamatory, expressive style, in instrumental music.

Parody Mass - A type of Mass flourishing in the 16th-century, based on musical material taken from another work by the same or another composer.

Partita *(It.)* A suite.

Part-writing - The technique of supplying the missing voices to any given voice or voices.

Pasodoble *(Sp.)* A modern Spanish dance in quick 2/4 meter.

Passacaglia *(It.)* Italian dance in triple meter written on a ground bass. A continuous variation based on a clearly distinguishable ostinato.

Passage - A term which is loosely used to refer to a short section of a composition.

Passepied *(Fr.)* An old French dance in 3/8 or 6/9 meter; a paspy.

Passing tone - A nonharmonic tone which conjunctly connects two harmonic tones, usually a third apart. *See* **THEORY - NONHAR-MONIC TONES.**

Passionato *(It.)* Very expressive, impassioned.

Passion Music - Music set to the narrative of our Lord's Passion in the Gospel.

Pastoral *(It.)* A scenic cantata; an instrumental piece depicting rural scenes.

Pastorale *(It.)* In pastoral style.

Patch cord - Sometimes called an attachment cord, a short cord or cable with a plug on both ends for conveniently connecting together two pieces of sound equipment.

Patetico *(It.)* With great emotion.

Pathetique *(Fr.)* Same as patetico.

Patter song - A humorous song, usually quite fast, sung inparlando style.

Pause *(Fr.,Ger.)* Rest. Also known as hold or fermata, indicating that the note or rest over which it appears is to be prolonged. *See* **THEORY - SIGNS.**

Pavane *(Fr.)* A stately dance in slow duple meter of Spanish origin.

Pedal-board - A keyboard played with the feet such as is normally found on the organ.

Pedal point - A sustained pedal or bass note, over which occur varying chords and harmonies. In modern usage, any tone or tones prolonged throughout changes in harmony. An organ point.

Pedal tone - A sustained or continuously repeated tone.

Pentatonic - A scale of five tones. Also used to describe the most common pentatonic order as revealed by the intervallic relationship of the black keys of the keyboard. *See* **THEORY - SCALES AND MODES.**

Percussion - Instruments that are struck, as a drum, bell, cymbals, etc.

Percussion ensemble - A self-contained performing ensemble made up solely of percussion instruments.

Perfect authentic cadence - A special cadence in which both the dominant and tonic chords have their roots in the bass and the soprano ascends or descends stepwise to the root of the tonic.

Perfect cadence - An arrangement of the V-I cadence in which the dominant and tonic chords are in root position and the tonic note in the soprano.

Perfect pitch - Absolute pitch. The faculty of a person to hear and identify a pitch by name without reference to another pitch.

Perfect plagal cadence - A plagal cadence in which the soprano note remains unchanged in the progression IV-I.

Period - A natural grouping of two phrases; a complete musical statement ending on a full close.

Perpetual canon - Like a round, a canon in which the final cadence leads back into the opening measures.

Peu a peu *(Fr.)* Gradually, little by little.

Philharmonic *(Gr.)* Loving harmony.

Phrase *(Fr.)* Phrased. A natural division of the melodic line comparable to a clause of speech; it must have a cadence. Complete in one sense if it is incomplete in another.

Phrasing - A system used in music to punctuate melodies much as a sentence is punctuated.

Phrygian - *See* **THEORY - SCALES AND MODES.**

Phrygian cadence - A harmonic close which originated in the Phrygian mode as the final cadence. In modern usage, any transposition of the progression IV6-V#.

Phrygian mode - Similar to the natural minor scale, however, its second degree is lowered one-half step. *See* **THEORY - SCALES AND MODES.**

Pianissimo *(It.)* Very soft. Also, pp.

Piano *(It.)* Soft. Also, *p* Common name for the pianoforte.

Piano, electronic - A keyboard instrument whose tones are produced by reeds, strings, or other means and amplified.

Piano quartet - A composition for piano, violin, viola, and cello.

Piano quintet - A composition for piano and string quartet.

Piano score - An arrangement of an orchestral work for piano.

Piano trio - A composition for piano, violin, and cello.

Piatti *(It.)* Cymbals.

Picardy third - The practice of ending a composition in the minor mode on a major chord by chromatically raising the third of the final chord in the perfect cadence.

Piccolo *(It.)* Small; an important flute stop in organs; a small flute pitched an octave higher than the orchestral flute, usually pitched in C but sometimes in D♭.

Pickup - The introductory note(s) leading into the first note of a tune. The anacrusis.

Piece - A musical composition. Sometimes used in reference to an instrument or to a member of an instrumental group.

Pinched - Harmonics on wind instruments created by overblowing or by the use of finger stops.

Pitch (acoustics) - The word used to indicate the relative highness or lowness of a tone. It is scientifically determined by the number of vibrations per second. *See* **THEORY - SIGNS.**

Pitch names - Designations used to indicate the various tones of pitches, e.g., within an octave C,D,E,F,G,A,B. The chromatic alterations, sharps and flats, are also included.

Pitch-pipe - A small reed-pipe which sounds tones of fixed pitch.

Piu *(It.)* More.

Piu mosso, piu moto *(It.)* More motion, quicker.

Pivot chord - The chord used in a modulation which is common to both keys.

Pizzicato *(It.)* Plucked.

Plagal cadence - The cadence progression from subdominant (IV) to tonic (I).

Plainsong - *See* **Gregorian Chant.**

Playback - The playing of a recorded tape or soundtrack after it has been recorded.

Plectrum *(Lat.)* A quill, or piece of ivory used to pluck the strings.

Poco a poco *(It.,Sp.)* Gradually, little by little.

Point d'orgue *(Fr.)* Pedal point.

Polarity - The attraction of a tone, an interval, or a complex of tones towards a given point.

Polka - A dance in 2/4 meter, originated among the peasants of Bohemia.

Polonaise *(Fr.)* A Polish dance in 3/4 meter and moderate tempo.

Polychord - A vertical sonority made up of two or more identifiable triads or seventh chords.

Polyphonic - Music which is conceived as a combination of two or more melodies rather than a succession of chords accompanying one melody.

Polyphony - Music for several voices in which the melodic lines prevail over the harmonic element. Music that is composed of parts, or voices, which support one another, in contrast with homophony, which is melody supported by chords.

Pomposo *(It.)* Majestic, stately.

Ponticello *(It.)* Bridge.

Pop - A popular number, a tune enjoying a success with the large public. If it stands the test of time, it becomes a "standard."

Portamento *(It.)* A type of ornamental resolution of a suspension. A glide from one note to another. In piano music, two or more notes under a slur, with dots above them, the notes to be played with some emphasis and separated slightly.

Portative - A small portable organ used in religious processions.

Portato *(It.)* Half-staccato, indicated by a dot with a short curved line over or under notes.

Position - See open and close structure. Also, the position of the left hand on the fingerboard of stringed instruments, hand position at the piano, etc.

Postlude *(Lat.)* A closing voluntary on the organ.

Poussez *(Fr.)* Up-bow.

Pp *(It.)* Abbreviation for pianissimo.

Praeludium *(Ger.)* Upper mordent. *See* **THEORY - MUSICAL ORNAMENTS**.

Preclassical - Music that followed the baroque music of the early 18th-century and preceded the classical music of the late 18th century.

Prelude - A musical introduction to a composition or drama.

Premier, premiere *(Fr.)* First.

Prepared piano - Altering the piano by placing such objects as bolts, clips, screws, etc., on the strings.

Pre-recorded tape - Tape recordings that are commercially available.

Prestissimo *(It.)* As fast as possible.

Presto *(It.)* Fast, faster than allegro, the fastest of the conventional tempos.

Prime (unison) - Two tones of the same pitch. The first note of the scale. Also, the basic form of a twelve-tone row which may be subjected to inversion, retrograde, retrograde-inversion, or transposition. *See* **THEORY - INTERVALS**.

Primo *(It.)* First, principal.

Processional - A hymn sung in church during the entrance of the choir and clergy.

Program music - Descriptive music intended to represent actual scenes of events or distinct moods or phases of emotion. Also known as programmatic music.

Programmed music - The generation of music by means of automatic high-speed digital computers.

Program notes - Descriptive, historical notes in concert or recital programs, record or cassette liners, etc., to assist the listener's understanding and enjoyment of the music and the musicians.

Progression - *See* **progress**. Movement from note to note is melodic progression; from chord to chord is harmonic progression.

Progressive jazz - Jazz which embraced some or all of the harmonic and rhythmic developments innovated c.1945; jazz music based on chord progressions, rather than on melodies.

Pronto *(Sp., It.)* Swiftly, promptly.

Psalm - A sacred song or hymn.

Psalter - The volume containing the Book of Psalms, often with music.

Psycho-acoustics - The study of sound and its complexity, and its realistic communication both physically and psychologically to man.

Publishing rights - The song rights acquired by a record company affiliated with a music publisher from an artist/song writer when he is signed to a recording contract. Also, the song rights acquired by one company from another.

Pulse - The underlying beat over which rhythm is superimposed.

Pure minor scale - The natural or pure minor scale differs from the major scale in that the third, sixth and the seventh degrees are lowered one-half step, both ascending and descending. *See* **THEORY - SCALES AND MODES**.

Qq

Quadrasonic sound reproduction - A system of sound reproduction involving four speakers, each operating from its own channel. Same as quadraphonic.

Quadrille *(Fr.)* A French dance, consisting of five movements, in 6/8 or 2/4 meter.

Quadruple meter - Regular grouping of the meter units by four. *See* **THEORY - METERS**.

Quadruplet - Group of four equal notes executed in the time of three or six of the same kind in the regular rhythm. *See* **THEORY - ARTIFICIAL RHYTHMIC GROUPINGS**.

Quality - The color of a tone; the difference between tones of the same pitch played on various instruments.

Quartal harmony - Chords by fourths.

Quarter-note - A unit of music notation that receives one pulsation when the lower unit of the meter signature is four, it receives one-fourth the value of a whole note. *See* **THEORY - NOTATION**.

Quarter rest - A rest equal in time value to a quarter note. *See* **THEORY - NOTATION**.

Quarter tone - Half a semitone; an interval often heard in non-Western music and sometimes used in modern compositions.

Quartet - A composition for four performers or, simply, four performers.

Quasi *(It.)* As if, almost.

Quickstep - A spirited march in 6/8 meter.

Quintal chord - In contemporary composition, a chord built in intervals of the fifth, sometimes the perfect fifth, as a method of avoiding tertian harmony.

Quintet - A composition for five performers or, simply, five performers.

Quintole *(Ger.)* Quintuplet - A group of five notes to be played in the time of four of the same value. *See* **THEORY - ARTIFICIAL RHYTHMIC GROUPINGS**.

Quintuple meter (simple or compound) - Any meter which has five beats to a measure. *See* **THEORY - NOTATION**.

Quintuplet - A group of five notes played in place of four. *See* **THEORY - ARTIFICIAL RHYTHMIC GROUPINGS**.

Quodibet *(Lat.)* A sort of Fantasia; a Dutch concert.

Rr

R - Abbreviation in English and German for right.

R & B - Rhythm and blues.

Racket - A wind instrument with a double reed, consisting of a short fat solid wooden cylinder with a number of interconnecting tubes bored out around its periphery and joined to each other to form a continuous channel which is connected to a central channel from which the sound emerges.

Radio Cologne - The first major electronic music studio was established in Cologne, Germany in 1951 by Dr. Herbert Eimert. Raga (Hin.) A generic term for a Hindu scale, built to create moods, and consisting of 5, 6, or 7 different notes.

Ragtime - In jazz, an early form, popular from c. 1896 to 1920, which included vocal and instrumental music with current emphasis on piano music.

Rallentando *(It.)* Becoming slower.

RAM (random access memory) - The operating part of a computer's memory. The user can access any part of this memory at random and order it to perform computations.

Range - The number of notes a particular voice may sing or an instrument may play, usually thought of in terms of highest note possible to lowest possible.

R and R - See rock 'n' roll.

Rap - Rhythmic speech. The term refers to a technique first used by disc jockeys on Black radio stations whereby they record fast, rhythmically spoken lyrics over an existing backing track.

Re *(It.)* The syllable used in singing, etc., the supertonic, the second note of the scale. *See* **degree.**

Real-time - A term used to denote composition time equivalent to performance time, as opposed to abstract or nonreal time, in which, due to notation requirements, conception and composition requires much more time than performance.

Recital - A concert usually restricted to solo or chamber music performances.

Recitative - Free in tempo and rhythm.

Recitative, measured - Occurs when the accompaniment proceeds while the voice declaims; a modern form of the recitative.

Recorder - A type of vertical flute used originally during the 15th-18th-centuries, which today is made of wood or plastic.

Reed - A thin strip of cane, wood, or metal which, when set in vibration by a current of air, produces a musical sound.

Refrain - The chorus at the end of every stanza of some songs.

Rehearsal - A general practice before a performance.

Register - The set of pipes controlled by a single stop, in organs; the whole compass or one of the sections of voices or instruments.

Registration - The combination of stops in organ playing.

Relative major - A major key is relative to that minor key, the tonic of which lies a minor third below its own.

Relative minor - A minor key is relative to that major key, the tonic of which lies a minor third above its own.

Relative pitch (acoustics) - The pitch of a tone in relation to a standard tone or a given key. The ability to recognize a relative interval is one of the most important requirements of a musician.

Religioso *(It.)* Devout, sacred.

Renaissance - The period from 1400 to 1600 in music history.

Repeat - A sign signifying that the music between ‖: and :‖ is to be repeated.

Repertoire *(Fr.)* The pieces or compositions which a player, singer, or group are able to perform publicly.

Reprise *(Fr.)* A repeat; the chorus of a song.

Requiem *(Lat.)* Rest. The first word in the Mass for the dead.

Resolution - The tendency of chords to progress toward a point of rest. The strict treatment of dissonance regarding the leaving of the dissonant interval.

Resonance (acoustics) - The transmission of vibrations from one vibrating body to another.

Resonator - An acoustical implement that serves to reinforce sounds by resonance.

Rest - A symbol used to indicate relative periods of silence. *See* **THEORY - NOTATION**.

Retard - Perform gradually more slowly; hold back the tempo.

Retrograde - Moving backwards.

Retrograde inversion - The combination of retrograde motion and inversion.

R.H. *(Ger.)* Abbreviation for right hand.

Rhapsody, rhapsodie - Brilliant composition of irregular form.

Rhythm - The principle of alternating tension and relaxation in the duration of tones. The interference of sounds against an underlying pulse.

Rhythm and blues - The precursor of early rock 'n' roll, a popular music which combined strong repetitive rhythms with simple melodies, harmonies and the blues. Also known as R and B.

Rhythm band - A musical activity in elementary schools in which children play various types of percussion instruments while the teacher plays the melody and harmony on the piano.

Rhythm, harmonic - The pattern of the distribution of chord changes in a phrase; the relationship of meter to harmonic progression.

Rhythmic reading - Reproducing at sight only the durations represented by the symbols in printed music.

Rhythm section - In jazz, that section consisting of piano, bass, drums, guitar and sometimes utility percussion player.

Ripieno *(It.)* A mixture stop in organs; the full orchestra in a concerto grosso.

Rit. - Abbreviation for ritardando.

Ritardando *(It.)* Becoming slower, Abbreviated as ritard, rit.

Ritenuto *(It.)* Held back, immediately slower.

Ritournelle *(Fr.)* Ritornello (It.) A short prelude, interlude or postlude to an air; an Italian folk song.

Rock - American popular music, primarily of the 1960's and '70's which was an outgrowth of rock 'n' roll of the '50's. Featuring vocals, drums, electronic instruments, and amplified keyboards and guitars, it encompassed soft rock, punk rock, jazz rock, mellow rock, acid rock, folk rock, and others.

Rock 'n' roll - A popular American music of the 1950's that was an outgrowth of the rhythm and blues style of the '30's and '40's. Featuring vocals, jazz-like instrumentation, and a heavy percussive beat, the blues harmonic structure was commonly used.

Rococo - An ornamental type of composition during the 18th-century.

Roll - A tremolo or trill on percussion instruments. *See* **THEORY - SIGNS**.

ROM (read only memory) - In computers, a non-volatile (permanent) memory system which can only be interpreted in a certain sequence.

Romance - Songs for voice or instruments usually in lyrical style.

Roman numerals - Figures to identify chords, e.g., I, II, III, IV, V, VI, VII.

Roman School - In the 16th-century, group of Roman composers who continued the style of sacred a cappella music established by Palestrina.

Romantic - The period from c. 1815 to c. 1900 in music history.

Rondeau *(Fr.)* A form of music frequent in monophonic songs of the 13th-century.

Rondo *(It.)* An instrumental piece characterized by the principal theme being repeated after each new theme is introduced.

Root - The generating note of a triad or any of its inversions or modifications. *See* **THEORY - CHORD INVERSIONS.**

Root bass - A bass formed by harmonies all of which are in root position.

Rosin - A gum, the exudation of certain trees, which, when properly prepared, is used to rub over the hair of a bow.

Rote - Routine, fixed mechanical way of doing something; an ability to perform music mechanically without thought or understanding.

Round - A vocal canon for two or more voices or instrumental lines at the unison or octave.

Row - See tone row and serial music.

Rhumba - A Cuban dance with emphasis primarily on rhythm.

Rubato *(It.)* Taking a portion of the time value from one note and giving it to another note within the same measure, without altering the duration of the measure as a whole.

Ss

S - Abbreviation for segno (sign); senza (without); sinistra (left); subito (suddenly). Also, set.

Sackbut - Ancient name for the trombone-bass trumpet.

Sackpfeife *(Ger.)* Bagpipe.

Sahft *(Ger.)* Soft, gentle.

Salsa - Modern Latin American dance which originated in Cuba and Puerto Rico and emigrated to the New York Puerto Rican community. Salsa, meaning sauce, is usually played in fast tempo in 4/4 meter with large Latin rhythm sections using claves, bomba, bongo and conga drums, guiro, maracas, timbales, etc.

Saltato *(It.)* Springing bow.

Samba - A popular Brazilian dance in 2/2 or 2/4 meter.

Sanctus *(Lat.)* A part of the Communion service in the Church of England and a part of the Mass in the Roman Catholic Church.

Sans *(Fr.)* Without.

Santille *(Fr.)* See Saltato, a style of bowing.

Saraband - A dance of Spanish origin utilizing two eight measure reprises in slow tempo in triple meter.

Sarrusophone - A brass wind-instrument with a double reed.

S.A.T.B. - The abbreviation for soprano, alto, tenor, and bass on the title pages of vocal scores.

Sax - A saxophone (soprano, alto, tenor, baritone, or bass).

Saxophone - A metal wind-instrument with single reed and clarinet-like mouthpiece, invented c. 1840 by Adolphe Sax of Belgium.

Scales and modes - *See* **THEORY - SCALES AND MODES**.

Scale degrees - Roman numeral designations for the notes of a scale, used particularly in harmonic analysis to denote the various tones of the scale as used as the basis of chords. I (tonic), II (supertonic), III (mediant), IV (subdominant), V (dominant), VI (submediant or super dominant), VII (leading tone or subtonic).

Scat singing - In jazz, a type of vocal performance in which a singer improvises, imitating sounds of musical instruments and/or using simple syllables or nonsensical words.

Scenario - The outline of an opera which includes the plot, the main characters, scenes, and the entrances and exits of singers.

Scherzando *(It.)* Playfully, jestingly.

Scherzo *(It.)* Referring to the tempo and mood of a scherzo movement; lively and brisk. Usually the third movement of a symphony.

Schnell *(Ger.)* Fast.

Schneller *(Ger.)* Faster.

Schola Cantorum - Schools for church song founded in the 4th century.

School - A method or system of teaching; a group of composers whose works mark an epoch in the history of music.

Scoop - In vocal music, a portamento from a lower tone rather than a firm, clean attack.

Scordatura *(It.)* For special effects, or to play unusual or difficult passages, tuning a string instrument differently than usual.

Score - A manner of writing music which shows all the parts of an ensemble arranged vertically; the conductors copy, e.g., full score, reduced score, piano score, etc.

Score, full - A complete score of all the parts of a composition, either vocal or instrumental, or both.

Score, piano - An arrangement for the piano of choral or instrumental music.

Sea chanty - A seafaring song.

Secco *(It.)* Simple, plain, unadorned.

Secondary dominant - The dominant chord of a chord on any degree of a scale. *See* **tonicization**.

Secondary triads - The supertonic, mediant, submediant, and subtonic chords of any major or minor key.

Second inversion chord - Occurs when the fifth of a triad is placed in the bass or lowest voice. *See* **THEORY - CHORD INVERSIONS**.

Second inversion seventh chord - Occurs when the fifth of the seventh chord is placed in the bass or lowest voice. *See* **THEORY - CHORD INVERSIONS**.

Segno *(It.)* Sign, meaning the sign.

Segue *(It.)* Continue without pausing.

Sehr *(Ger.)* Very.

Sel-sync - In tape recording, an electronic circuit that is used to synchronize the recording of a new track with previously recorded material on other tracks. Abbreviation for selective synchronization.

Semi *(Lat.)* Half.

Semi-acoustical guitar - A guitar with a hollow resonating body and the appropriate electrical attachments which may be played electrically or acoustically.

Semiquaver - A sixteenth note. *See* **THEORY - NOTATION**.

Semitone - The half of a whole tone; the smallest interval of European music.

Semplice *(It.)* Simple, unaffected.

Sempre *(It.,Port.)* Continually, always, throughout.

Senza *(It.)* Without.

Septet - A musical group containing seven performers.

Septuplet - A group of seven equal notes to be played in the time of four or six of the same kind in the regular rhythm. *See* **THEORY - ARTIFICIAL RHYTHMIC GROUPINGS**.

Sequence - A systematic transposition of a motive to different scale degrees. It may be literal (modulating) or diatonic (non- modulating).

Serenade - An instrumental or vocal composition short or rather simple in character.

Serialized harmony - In twelve-tone music, harmonic structures derived from a tone row.

Serial music - Term used interchangeably with twelve-tone music and dodecaphonic music. Music based on a series of notes chosen from the twelve tones of the chromatic scale. Such a series, or row, functions in some ways as a scale does in tonal music in that it serves as the raw material out of which the compositon is made.

Serious music - Classical music.

SESAC - A performing-rights organization. Unlike ASCAP and BMI, it is a privately owned profit-making corporation.

Seulement *(Fr.)* Only.

Seventh - The interval located seven diatonic steps away from the prime.

Seventh chord - A seventh chord is a four-tone chord built in thirds above a given root. Its name is derived from the interval formed between the root, third and seventh when the chord is in root position. *See* **THEORY - CHORD TYPES**.

Sextet - A music group of six performers.

Sforzando *(It.)* With a strong accent.

Shake - A trill. In jazz, a note executed with pronounced vibrato, almost a trill, especially by trumpets and trombones. Often used to link one chorus to another or at the beginining of a phrase. *See* **THEORY - JAZZ ARTICULATION.**

Shanty - In past times, song of the English working class.

Shaped notes - A form of notation in the mid-19th-century in which each note had a unique shape to identify its position on the scale. This notation is still used in some sections of the country in the performance of sacred and semi-sacred music.

Sharp - The notation (#) placed before the head of a note raises its pitch one-half tone. As an adjective, too high in pitch.

Sharp, double - The sign (x) which raises the pitch of a note one whole step.

Sharped tone - Raises the pitch one-half step.

Shift - In string playing, a change of position.

Shofar - An ancient Jewish trumpet made from a ram's horn.

Show group - A performing group that is capable of doing routines that have a special entertainment value. A show group as opposed to a dance group.

Shuffle - A dance created in the south, later applied to a boogie-woogie type rhythm, slow and strongly syncopated.

Shuffle rhythm - In commercial music, a rhythm pattern consisting of dotted eighth and sixteenth notes, played continuously in a monotonous pattern.

Si *(It.)* The syllable used to denote the seventh note of the scale. *See* **degrees**.

Side drum - The snare drum; the most commonly used drum in instrumental music.

Sideman - A player in a music ensemble, as differentiated from the leader or conductor.

Sight reading - Reading a piece of music without rehearsal or specific preparation.

Sight singing - Reading and singing a piece of music without rehearsal or specific preparation.

Signal horn - A bugle.

Similar motion - Two parts moving in the same direction, but not necessarily the same distance.

Simile *(It.)* In like manner, similarly.

Simple beat - A beat which has a background of two equal pulsations. *See* **THEORY - CONDUCTING FRAMES**.

Simple meter - *See* simple beat. *See* **THEORY - METERS**.

Sinfonia *(It.)* A symphony or opera-overture.

Singing - The development of the technique of the use of the voice in song.

Singspiel *(Ger.)* An 18th-century type of German opera, light with spoken interludes.

Sinistra *(It.)* Left.

Sitar - A popular Indian instrument, shaped like a lute, and plucked with a plectrum.

Six-four chord - The second inversion of a triad. *See* **THEORY - CHORD INVERSIONS**.

Six, Les *(Fr.)* Six French composers led by Eric Satie in the 1920's who shared an opposition to the vagueness of impressionism and an allegiance to simplicity and neoclassicism. They were Georges Auric, Louis Durey, Arthur Honegger, Darius Milhaud, Francois Poulenc, and Germaine Tailleferre.

Sixteenth - An interval of two octaves and a second.

Sixteenth note - A unit of music notation that receives one-half the time value of an eighth note. A semiquaver. *See* **THEORY - NOTATION**.

Sixteenth rest - A pause equal in duration to a sixteenth note. *See* **THEORY - NOTATION**.

Sixth - The interval located six diatonic steps above the prime.

Sixth chord - The first inversion of a triad. *See* **THEORY - CHORD INVERSIONS**.

Sixth chord, augmented - Italian sixth, French sixth, and German sixth. *See* **THEORY - SIXTH CHORDS**.

Sixth chord, Neapolitan - A chord built on the lowered supertonic in first inversion. *See* **THEORY - SIXTH CHORDS**.

Sizzle cymbal - A regular cymbal with a number of small jingles or sizzlers attached to the upper surface which, when played, produces a sizzling sound.

Slap - To pluck the bass string so that it hits against the neck of the bass producing a slapping effect.

Slide - A moveable tube in the trombone. Also, to pass from one note to another without any cessation of sound.

Slur - A curved line drawn over two or more notes to indicate that they are to be played legato. *See* **THEORY - SIGNS**.

Smear - Glissando. In jazz, a smear is indicated by a wavy line over the note, instructing the player to approach a tone from below and slide into it. *See* **THEORY - JAZZ ARTICULATION**.

Snare drum - A side drum with heads on both top and bottom; the top is played upon while the snares, stretched across the bottom, vibrate against the head to reinforce the tone.

Soave *(It.)* Sweet, delicate, gentle.

Sociology of music - The study of the relationship between music and society.

Soft rock - Rock music popular in the 1960's emanating in California, featuring a lighter, looser and more airy feeling than other rock styles.

Sol-fa - Refers to the singing of solfeggi to the solmization syllables.

Solfege *(Fr.)* Syllables of solmization of the scale such as do, re, mi, fa, sol, la, ti (si), do.

Solo, soli *(It., Lat., Sp.)* Alone, single, a part performed by one performer; a term for various stops of more conspicuous tone color than the average rank of the same name, in organs.

Sonare *(It.)* To sound, to play upon.

Sonata *(It.)* An instrumental composition, usually for a solo instrument, in three or four contrasting, extended movements.

Sonata-allegro form - A ternary form usually applied in the first movement of a sonata. It usually deals with two or three themes set in the form of exposition, development, and recapitulation.

Sonata da camera, sonata da chiesa *(It.)* Chamber sonata, church sonata.

Sonata form - Form used for the first movements of symphonies from the classical period, as well as sonatas and chamber works.

Sonatina *(It.)* Sonatine *(Fr.)* A short sonata usually in two or three movements, sometimes written as one long movement.

Song - A short poem with musical setting.

Song cycle - A group of related songs that form a musical entity.

Song form - A vocal or instrumental composition comprised of two, three or more sections.

Sonority - The quality of sound including loudness, fullness, resonance, and projection.

Sopra *(It.)* Above, over.

Soprano *(It.)* The highest voice in a four-part composition. The highest female voice.

Sordino *(It.)* Mute or damper.

Sostenuto *(It.)* Sustained.

Sostenuto pedal - The third pedal on some pianos, usually grand, that sustain only those tones whose dampers are already raised by the action of the keys.

Sotto voce *(It.)* Softly, in a low voice.

Soul - A style of singing which began with rhythm and blues and continued until the present day.

Sound-board - The general term for the piece of fir or other resonant wood used in the construction of various stringed and keyboard instruments.

Sound hole - A hole, or holes, cut in the belly of a string instrument which allows the sound to be transmitted.

Sound post - A small post, or prop, within a string instrument.

Sousaphone - A tuba of spiral shape, which is coiled around the player with the bell pointing forwards. It is named after John Philip Sousa, the march king.

Spacing - The vertical arrangement of the notes of a chord.

Speakeasy - A night club in the 1920's.

Special - An exclusive arrangement, belonging to one group only.

Species - The name given to each of five types of academic strict counterpoint, progressively more complex, i.e., first species, second species, etc.

Spiccato *(It.)* A light staccato played between the frog and the midpoint of the bow, at slow to moderate speed, in bowing.

Spirito *(It.)* Spirit, fire, energy.

Spiritoso *(It.)* Lively, spirited.

Spiritual - A religious song cultivated in the 19th-century by Black slaves in the South.

Sprechstimme *(Ger.)* Speech song, inflected spoken singing, with pitches indicated approximately on the music staff.

Springing bow - A style of bowing in which the bow is allowed to bounce on the strings.

Square dance - A country dance performed by several couples in a square formation.

Staccato *(It.)* Detached, with each note separated from the next and quickly released. A manner of performance indicated by a dot placed over the note, calling for a reduction of its written duration with a rest substituted for half or more of its value.

Staff (stave) - A series of horizontal equal distant lines, now five in number, upon which music notes are written.

Staff notation - Music notation employing a staff as distinct from staffless notations, e.g., tonic sol-fa and earlier systems using figures, letters, or other symbols.

Standard pitch - In May, 1939, at the International Conference on Pitch, held in London, a1 = 440 vibrations per second was unanimously adopted as the standard pitch.

Stanza - A symmetric unit of a song.

Static harmony - An absence of root change in a harmonic progression.

Steel band - Bands in the Caribbean, playing calypso and reggae rhythms, which use steel oil drums as the principal rhythm instruments.

Steel guitar - An electrophonic instrument in which the sound is produced by an electric pickup system, with an amplifier contained in a separate cabinet connected by cable to the pickup. It is tuned like the acoustic guitar but its body may take many shapes.

Step - The interval between two contiguous degrees of a scale.

Stereophonic - More than single-channel recording.

Stock (arrangement) - A published commercial arrangement usually simplified and standardized.

Stop chorus, stop time - A chorus in which the orchestra plays only one note in every one or two measures as a background for a tap dancer or other soloist. A solo chorus for any intrument or for voice, played with no accompaniment except a periodic pulsing accent by the other instruments generally on the first beat of every measure or alternate measures.

Stop diapason - In organs, a stop in which the pipes are generally made of wood and its bass, up to middle C, always made of wood.

Storyville - The famous New Orleans legalized brothel district from 1896-1917, where many of the early jazz musicians first played and introduced jazz music.

Stradivarius - Named for the maker, Antonio Stradivari in Cremona, Italy, one of the most famous violins made from the 18th-century to the present day.

Street, The Swing Street (or Alley) - During the swing era (c.1935-1945) in New York City, 52nd Street between 5th and 7th Avenues, where small jazz night clubs flourished.

Stretto *(It.)* Accelerated, faster; a concluding section in faster tempo; the device of speeding up imitation by the various parts, contrapuntal music.

Strict counterpoint - An academic discipline employed in teaching beginning counterpoint, based on the melodic and harmonic materials of pre-17th-century vocal composition.

String - Prepared wire, silk, catgut or plastic, plain or covered, used for musical instruments. In a computer program, a string of numbers or letters grouped together.

String bass - Colloquial name for the double bass.

Stringed instruments - Instruments whose tones are produced by strings, bowed, plucked, or struck.

String quartet - A composition in four parts for two violins, viola and cello. The players comprising the quartet.

String trio - A composition for 3 stringed instruments, normally violin, viola, and cello.

Strobe tuner - An electronic instrument tuner which utilizes stroboscopic light.

Strophic form - Form in which the same music is repeated for each verse.

Studio musician - A musician who specializes in recording masters.

Subdominant (fa) - Referring to the fourth degree of the scale. *See* **Degrees**.

Subdominant chord - Any chord built on the fourth degree of the diatonic scale. *See* **THEORY - CHORD TYPES.**

Subito *(It.)* Suddenly, at once, immediately.

Subject - Theme. A melodic motive or phrase on which a composition is founded.

Submediant (la) - Referring to the sixth degree of a diatonic scale. *See* **degrees**.

Suboctave - The octave below a given tone.

Suite *(Fr.)* A series or set of movements in various dance forms.

Sul, sulla, sulle *(It.)* On the.

Sul ponticello *(It.)* Near the bridge.

Sul tasto *(It.)* On the fingerboard.

Superdominant - The sixth degree of a diatonic scale. *See* **submediant**.

Superimposition - The placing of one chord structure over another.

Supertonic (re) Referring to the second degree of the scale. *See* **degrees**.

Sur *(Fr.)* On, over.

Suspension - Highly important as a means of emotional expression, particularly in its relationship to the principle of tension and release. A melodic device delaying the entrance of an expected tone; also, the delaying (or suspended) tone itself. *See* **THEORY - NONHARMONIC TONES**.

Suzuki method - A method conceived by Shinichi Suzuki of Japan which instructs young children to play music (particularly the violin) by ear and to recall what is heard prior to reading printed music.

Swing - In jazz, the swing era was synonymous with the big band era in the 1930's and featured well-rehearsed and well-written compositions and arrangements for a full complement of saxophones, trumpets, trombones, piano, guitar, bass and drums. Individual solos were featured as well as the full ensemble sound, Also, to "feel" the beat, to propel.

Swing era - The period during the 1930's and '40's when the big bands were the popular music of the day.

Symphonic poem - A musical illustration or setting of an episode or story.

Symphony - An orchestral composition usually containing the following movements or movements of similar relationships: I. Allegro, II. Adagio, III. Scherzo, IV. Allegro. Also, an instrumental ensemble comprised of strings, woodwinds, brass, and percussion.

Syncopate - To efface or shift the accent from a strong beat to a weak beat.

Syncopation - The deliberate upsetting of the normal pulse of meter, accent and rhythm.

Synthesizer - An electronic instrument which uses filters, oscillators, and amplifiers to produce sounds not obtainable from conventional musical instruments.

System - Where two or more portions of a score appear on one page, each such portion (suggested either by a space or two short parallel lines ||) is called a system.

Tt

T - Abbreviation for taste, tempo, tenor, tonic, tutti, and toe (in organ music). Also, the letter T is used to identify a twelve-tone row or segment of a row that has been moved to a new pitch level.

Tablature *(Fr.)* A general name for all the signs and characters used in music; also, a peculiar system of notation used for instruments of the string class and certain wind instruments.

Tabor - A small drum tapped with one hand, accompanying a folk singer.

Tacet *(Lat.)* Be silent. Parts are marked tacet in instrumental or choral music which are not wanted for a movement or section.

Tag - In jazz, a musical phrase added to the end of a chorus or performance.

Tailgate, tail-gate - In jazz, the New Orleans style of trombone playing originated when brass bands playing ragtime or early jazz were loaded onto advertising trucks and the trombonist, in order to give free play to the full length of the slide, had to stand near the tailgate of the truck.

Tambour de Basque *(Fr.)* Tambourine.

Tambourine - An instrument of the drum class, formed of a hoop of wood or metal, over which is stretched a piece of skin. The sides of the hoop are pierced with holes, into which are inserted metal jingles.

Tam-tam *(It., Fr., Ger.)* Gong.

Tango *(Sp.)* Popular Argentinian dance in duple meter.

Tanto *(It.)* Much, as much, so much.

Tarantella *(It.)* An Italian dance in 6/8 meter.

Tardamente *(It.)* Lingeringly, slowly.

Tardando *(It.)* Retarding, delaying.

Tardo *(It.)* Serious, slow; delayed, late.

Tasto *(It.)* Fingerboard, key, fret.

Technique *(Fr.)* The mechanical skill which is the foundation of the mastery of an instrument, voice, or type of composition.

Te Deum *(Lat.)* We praise.

Tema *(It.)* Theme, subject.

Temperament - The division of the scale into semitones. Those systems of tuning in which the intervals deviate from the acoustically correct intervals used in the Pythagorian system.

Temple block - A hollow block of resonant wood played by striking with a drumstick. Also called Korean temple block or Chinese block.

Tempo *(It.)* Rate of speed, time.

Tempo comodo *(It.)* Convenient speed.

Tempo mark - A phrase or word which indicates the rate of speed at which a composition, movement, or piece should be played.

Tempo rubato *(It.)* Irregular time.

Tenor - In part music, the part above the lowest. The highest natural voice of men.

Tenor drum - A percussion instrument similar to the side drum but deeper in pitch, bigger, and without snares.

Tenor trombone - The B-flat trombone.

Tenuto *(It.)* Held, sustained.

Ternary form - Music which is divided into three parts.

Tertian harmony - Chords by thirds.

Tessitura *(It.)* The location of a majority of tones in a piece or song. A high tessitura refers to extremes of the soprano register, a low tessitura to extremes of the bass register of any given voice or instrument.

Tetrachord - A succession of four tones which is the basis for constructing a scale. Two disjunct tetrachords make up one scale. In twelve-tone music, four adjacent notes of a set or row, especially the first, second, or third group within the group of twelve.

Texture - The horizontal and vertical relationships of musical materials including monophonic, homophonic, polyphonic, and hybrid.

Theme - A subject; a musical motto which serves as the basis of a composition or movement.

Theme and variations - A composition in which the principal theme is stated at the beginning followed by several variations.

Theory of music - The science of music. *See* **THEORY.**

Theremin - An electronic instrument invented by and named for the Russian scientist Leon Theremin c. 1924.

Third - The third degree of the diatonic scale and the interval thus formed. *See* **THEORY - INTERVALS**.

Third inversion seventh chord (4/2) - A chord in which the seventh of the seventh chord is placed in the bass or lowest voice. *See* **THEORY - CHORD INVERSIONS**.

Third stream, third-stream, thirdstream - In the 1950's, the fusing of jazz and contemporary music by some jazz composers and performers.

Thirty-second note - A note having three flags attached to its stem receiving half the value of a sixteenth note. *See* **THEORY NOTATION**.

Thorough-bass - A method of indicating an accompanying part by the bass notes together with figures designating the chief intervals and accompanying harmony. *See* **figured bass**.

Through-composed - Opposite of strophic. A song that has new music composed for each stanza.

Ti - A syllable sometimes used for the seventh note of the scale, in place of si, which is too sibilant. *See* **degrees**.

Tie - A curved line placed over a note and its repetition to show that the two shall be performed as one unbroken note.

Time - Customarily used for meter, i.e., the number of beats in a bar, as 3/4 time, 4/4 time, etc. It is more specific to use the word meter instead of time, to avoid confusion with tempo.

Time signature - *See* **meter signature**.

Timpani *(It.)* Kettledrums, timpani.

Tin-Pan Alley - A designation for the industry, centered in New York City, which published popular music.

Toccata *(It.)* A touch piece, any keyboard piece.

Tom-tom - An American Indian drum. In jazz, a pair of tuned drums, normally placed between the bass drum and the snare drum with the larger ones on the floor and the smaller ones mounted on the bass drum.

Tonal - Pertaining to a tone, key, or mode,

Tonal and real - An answer is called real if it is an exact transposition of the subject and tonal if certain intervals are changed, in a fugue.

Tonality - All notes in the scale related to one central tone; includes all harmony related to a given tonic chord. It may include major and parallel minor keys. The totality of the melodic and harmonic elements of a musical work, as related to a common tonal center.

Tone - The building material of music. A tone possesses pitch, loudness, timbre and duration. It is produced by a regular vibration of an elastic body.

Tone clusters - Three or more adjacent tones sounding simultaneously.

Tone color - Tone quality.

Tone poem - 19th and 20th-century orchestral compositions based on programmatic or poetic ideas.

Tone row - An arbitrary arrangement of the twelve chromatic tones.

Tonguing - Producing various tone effects on wind instruments by using the tongue. Players may attack, single tongue, double tongue, triple tongue, etc.

Tonic (do) - The keynote of a scale; the first degree of the scale. *See* **degrees**.

Tonicization - The process whereby harmonies other than the tonic are given greater vividness or emphasis.

Tono *(It.)* Tone, whole tone, key.

Torch song - In the 1930's and '40's, a ballad sung by a singer who "carried the torch" for someone.

Tosto *(It.)* Quick.

Touch - The art of depressing the piano keys so as to produce a musical tone. Also, the resistance of the piano keyboard.

Touche *(Fr.)* Key, fingerboard of a stringed instrument.

Tr. *(It.)* Abbreviation for trillo.

Traditional jazz - Jazz of the early 20th-century, e.g., Dixieland.

Transcription - An arrangement of a piece for some voice or instrument, or combination other than that for which it was originally intended.

Transition - Modulation, passing modulation.

Transpose - To write or perform a piece in a different key.

Transposing instruments - Instruments whose parts require a transposition from the true sounding pitches. Instruments have usually been transposed to bring about a standard system of fingering for instruments of the same family, e.g., saxophones or clarinets, which differ widely in range.

Transposition - The process of shifting music from one tonality to another.

Transverse flute - *See* **cross flute**.

Tre *(It.)* Three.

Treble clef - The soprano or "G" clef. *See* **THEORY - CLEFS.**

Tremolando *(It.)* Rippling, trembling, quivering.

Tremolo *(It.)* A slight steady wavering of pitch. On stringed instruments the quick reiteration of the same tone. In singing, a slight fluctuation of pitch. In keyboard music, the rapid alternation of two or more pitches. *See* **THEORY - SIGNS.**

Triad - Fundamental harmony consisting of root, third and fifth (major, minor, augmented, diminished). *See* **THEORY - CHORD TYPES.**

Trill - A musical ornament consisting of the rapid alternation of a given note with the diatonic second above it. *See* **THEORY - MUSICAL ORNAMENTS.**

Trio *(It.)* A piece for three parts or three voices. Three performers. Also, the division between the first theme and its repetition in marches and minuets.

Trio sonata - Baroque chamber music with two upper voices and a thorough bass.

Triple meter - Regular groupings of time units by three.

Triplet - A group of three notes to be performed in the place of two of the same kind, indicated by a three and usually a bracket. *See* **THEORY - ARTIFICIAL RHYTHMIC GROUPINGS.**

Tritone - The interval of three whole tones, the augmented fourth or diminished fifth, a strong dissonance. *See* **Diabolus in Musica.**

Trombone - A metal wind-instrument of the trumpet family. It consists of two tubes, sliding in and out of the other.

Troppo *(It.)* Too, too much.

Troubadours - Poet-musicians in Spain, Italy and France from the 11th-century until the end of the 13th-century.

Trumpet - A metal wind-instrument with cupped mouthpiece, small bell, and three valves. An 8' reed stop of powerful tone, in organs.

Tuba *(It.,Sp.)* Tuba, bass tuba; trumpet; the lowest pitched instrument in the brass family. Also, a name for various chorus reed stops with a firmer tone quality than the trompette or trumpet stops, in organs.

Tubular chimes - Metal bells made of long, hollow cylindrical tubes, suspended from a bar.

Tune - An air, melody. Also the act of adjusting the pitch of an instrument.

Tuning - The adjustment of an instrument to a recognized pitch.

Tuning-fork - A two-pronged instrument of metal, which upon being struck, gives a certain fixed tone; used for tuning instruments.

Tuning head - *See* **machine head**.

Turn - An ornament consisting of a group of four or five notes which wind around the principal note. A grupetto. *See* **THEORY - MUSICAL ORNAMENTS**.

Tutta, tutte, tutti *(It.)* All, total; full orchestra or full chorus.

Twelve-tone technique - A system of composition in which the twelve chromatic tones are considered important and are related one to another.

Two-part form - *See* **binary form**.

Two step - A fast American ballroom dance popular in the early 1900's.

Tympani - Timpani.

Uu

U - Abbreviation of the German word und (and).

Ukulele - A popular, small, guitar-like instrument with strings tuned G-C-E-A, which developed in Hawaii in the 19th-century from the Portuguese machete.

Una corda *(It.)* Soft pedal. Also, in string playing, on one string only.

Underscoring - A dramatic background score (composition) for a motion picture.

Unequal temperament - Any system of tuning between pure intonation and equal temperament.

Unequal voices - Mixture of men's and women's voices.

Unis *(Fr.)* In unison.

Unison (prime) - Two tones with the same letter name, sounding the same pitch. *See* **THEORY - INTERVALS**.

Unordered set - In twelve-tone music, a collection of notes with no specified succession.

Un peu *(Fr.)* A little.

Un poco *(It.)* A little.

Unpublished copyright - As defined by the Copyright Office, an unpublished copyright is generally one for which copies have not been sold, placed on sale, or made available to the public.

Unruhig *(Ger.)* Restless.

Up-beat - One or several initial notes of a melody which occur before the first bar line. *See* **anacrusis.** Also, the second or last beat in a bar.

Up-bow - The stroke of a stringed instrument bow from point to nut.

Upright piano - As distinguished from a grand piano, an instrument with its strings arranged diagonally along the vertical soundboard. Small upright pianos are called spinets.

Ut *(Fr.)* The syllable used by the French, in instrumental music, instead of do, to designate the first note of the scale, or C.

Ut supra *(Lat.)* As above, as before.

Vv

V - An abbreviation for verte, vide, violin, volti, and voce.

Valse *(Fr.)* Waltz.

Valve - In brass wind instruments, a device by means of which brass tubes may be made to sound the semitones and tones between the natural open harmonics.

Valve trombone - A trombone utilizing three piston valves instead of a slide.

Valve trumpet - The modern trumpet.

Valzer *(It.)* Waltz.

Vamp - In jazz, an old expression meaning to improvise an accompaniment.

Variation - A transformation of a theme by means of harmonic, rhythmic or melodic changes.

Variety show - A stage show consisting of several performers, each with a different performance ability.

Vaudeville *(Fr.)* Light comedy, combining dialogue, pantomime, with popular tunes performed until the middle of the 20th-century.

Venetian school - A 16th-century school of Italian and Flemish composers active in Venice and best represent by Giovanni Gabrieli (1557-1612).

Veranderungen *(Ger.)* Changes, variations.

Verhallend *(Ger.)* Fading away.

Verse - A stanza. Also, an introductory section of a popular song, as distinguished from the chorus. The latter consists most commonly of thirty-two bars, while the verse may have an irregular number of bars and may be sung or played in a free tempo.

Vertical sonority - Any combination of notes sounded simultaneously.

Via sordino *(It.)* Take off mute.

Vibes - The abbreviation used to cover all instruments of which the manufacturing company trade names are "vibraphone," "vibraharp," "vibrabells," etc.

Vibraharp - The vibraphone.

Vibraphone - A percussion instrument with metal bars suspended in a keyboard arrangement over resonator tubes. When the motor-driven mechanism beneath the resonator tubes is activated, and the bars are struck with mallets, vibrato occurs.

Vibration (acoustics) Rapid oscillations of a sounding body, e.g., strings, columns of air, etc.

Vibrato *(It.)* Pulsation of musical sound, reverberating, resounding ringing. On stringed instruments, the slight fluctuation of pitch produced on sustained notes by an oscillating motion of the left hand. In singing and wind instrument playing a scarcely noticeable wavering of tone.

Viennese School - Refers to two schools of composers centered in Austria. The first, the Classical Viennese School, included Beethoven, Haydn, Mozart, Schubert, and others. The latter, the 20th-century Viennese School, refers to Schoenberg and other twelve-tone composers.

Vigoroso *(It.)* Boldly, vigorously, energetically.

Viol *(Sp.)* An old instrument similar to the violin, but a little larger with six strings. Also, the name for a family of bowed stringed instruments of the 16th and 17th-centuries.

Viola *(It.)* A bowed string instrument with its 4 strings, C, G, D, A, tuned a fifth lower than the violin. The alto instrument of the violin group.

Violin *(Sp.)* Violin. The bowed soprano instrument of the string family, with 4 strings tuned G, D, A, and E.

Violin family - Violin, viola, cello, and double bass.

Violoncello *(It.)* A four-stringed bow instrument, tuned C, G, D and A, shaped like a violin and held, while playing, between the knees. Also an important string stop with the tone of the orchestral cello, in organs.

Virginal - A stringed instrument played by means of a keyboard like the piano. A small harpsichord.

Virtuoso *(It.)* Technically very difficult, brilliant. Also, a great artist-performer, instrumentally or vocally.

Vivace *(It.)* A lively tempo, somewhat faster than allegro.

Vivo *(Sp.)* Intense, lively.

Vl - Abbreviation for violin.

Vla - Abbreviation for viola.

Vlc - Abbreviation for violoncello, commonly referred to as cello.

Vll - Abbreviation for violins.

Vocal - Belonging to one voice; music intended to be sung. Also, a musical arrangement which includes a part for voice and that vocal performance.

Vocalese - Words fitted to a previously recorded instrumental line.

Vocalise *(Fr.)* Vocalizzo *(It.)* Vocalization, solfeggio.

Vocalization - The manner of singing.

Voce *(It.)* The voice.

Voice - The sound produced by the human organs of speech. Also, one of the parts in a composition.

Voice leading - In polyphonic music, the principles governing the progression of the various voice parts, particularly of those other than the soprano.

Voicing - The arrangement of voices in a vertical harmonic structure. Also, the mechanical adjustments necessary in order to obtain and maintain the proper tone color throughout a rank of pipes, in organs. The rehabilitation of the hammer felts, necessary in order to obtain an even quality of sound, in pianos.

Voile *(Fr.)* Veiled, subdued; a husky tone in singing.

Voix *(Fr.)* Voice or voice-part.

Voix humaine *(Fr.)* Same as vox humana in organs.

Volti *(It.)* Turn.

Volti subito *(It.)* Turn the page quickly. *See* **THEORY - SIGNS.**

Volume (acoustics) - The effect caused by the amplitude of the sound wave. The greater the displacement, the greater the volume or intensity, and vice versa.

Voluntary - An organ solo played before, during, or after any office of the church.

Vorspiel *(Ger.)* A prelude.

Vox *(Lat.)* Voice or voice-part.

V.S. *(It.)* Abbreviation for volti subito. Turn over quickly.

Ww

Wagner tuba - A brass instrument in two sizes, tenor and bass, used by Wagner in his music dramas.

Wah wah pedal - A pedal-operated device used to alter the sound of instruments electronically. It is used most often on the guitar and makes a sound like a baby crying.

Waldhorn *(Ger.)* A forest or hunting horn, a French horn. Also a reed stop designed to sound like a hunting horn, in organs.

Wallpaper music - Isolated phrases repeated over and over again like the pattern of wallpaper; sometimes referred to as "pedestrian" music.

Waltz - A round dance in triple meter.

Wehmutig *(Ger.)* Sad, melancholy.

Well-tempered - In equal temperament.

West coast jazz (or school sound) - A popular jazz style during the 1950's which was characterized by restraint, intellectuality and a studied relaxation.

Whistle - The sound produced through a small aperture in the lips; the pitch is governed by the shaping of the mouth as a resonating chamber.

Whole note - A note equal in value to twice that of a half note. In 4/4 meter, the whole note receives 4 beats. *See* **THEORY - NOTATION**.

Whole rest - A pause equal in length to a whole note. *See* **THEORY - NOTATION**.

Whole tone - A major second. *See* **THEORY - SCALES AND MODES**.

Whole-tone scale - A scale composed of only six tones, a whole step from each other. *See* **THEORY - SCALES AND MODES**.

Wind band - A band comprised of wind instruments and, usually, percussion.

Wind ensemble - An instrumental group comprised of the wind sections of the symphony orchestra, with percussion, double bass, and sometimes harp.

Wind instruments - Musical instruments whose sounds are produced by the breath of the player, or by means of bellows.

Wind machine - A percussion device consisting of a barrel framework covered with cloth and revolved so that the cloth is in friction with the wood of the framework to imitate the sound of wind. Today the sound is more realistically produced with synthesizers.

Wood block - Temple block.

Woodwinds - The flutes, oboes, clarinets, bassoons, saxophones and similar instruments in an instrumental performing group.

Word painting - Using musical means to illustrate non-musical ideas.

Wuchtig *(Ger.)* Slow, ponderous.

Wurdig *(Ger.)* Dignified, stately.

Xx

Xylomarimba - A large xylophone that covers the ranges of both the xylophone and marimba.

Xylophone - A percussion instrument, consisting of wooden bars tuned to the tones of the scale, and struck with mallets.

Yy

Yo *(In.)* An Indian flute.

Yodel or jodel - The peculiar warbling of the Swiss or Tyrolean mountaineers.

Yuehchyn *(Chi.)* A Chinese guitar.

Zz

Zamba - Originating in Peru, an Argentine and Chilean dance in fast 6/8 meter.

Zapateado *(Sp.)* Spanish dance in triple meter.

Zeitmass *(Ger.)* Tempo.

Ziemlich *(Ger.)* Rather.

Zimbel *(Ger.)* Cymbal; a brilliant mixture stop made up of open metal foundation pipes, in organs.

Zink *(Ger.)* The cornett, which is obsolete; a pedal reed stop in organs.

Zither *(Ger.)* A flat stringed instrument.

Zusammen *(Ger.)* In unison.

Zwei *(Ger.)* Two.

Zweistimmig *(Ger.)* For two voices.

Zwischenspiel *(Ger.)* Intermezzo, interlude.

Zymbel *(Ger.)* Cymbal.

Zwolftonmusik *(Ger.)* Twelve-tone music.

MUSICIANS
Aa

Acuff, Roy *(1903-1992)* American country-music singer and fiddler.

Adams, Pepper *(1930-1986)* American jazz baritone saxophonist.

Adderley, Julian "Cannonball" *(1928-1975)* American alto saxophonist.

Adler, Samuel *(1928-)* American composer.

Albeniz, Isaac *(1860-1909)* Spanish pianist and composer.

Alberti, Domenico *(1710-1740)* Italian harpsichordist and composer.

Allen, Steve *(1921-)* American pianist, songwriter, and comic.

Alpert, Herb *(1935-)* American trumpet player and composer.

Amram, David *(1930-)* American composer.

Anderson, Leroy *(1908-1975)* American composer.

Anderson, Marian *(1902-1993)* American contralto.

Antheil, George *(1900-1959)* American composer.

Argento, Dominick *(1927-)* American opera composer.

Arlen, Harold (Hyman Arluck) *(1905-1986)* American composer of musicals and films.

Arnold, Eddy *(1918-)* American country-music singer and guitarist.

Arnold, Malcolm *(1921-)* English composer.

Arrau, Claudio *(1903-)* Chilean pianist.

Atkins, Chet *(1924-)* American country-western guitarist.

Auer, Leopold *(1845-1930)* Hungarian violinist-pedagogue.

Austin, Frederic *(1872-1952)* English composer.

Ax, Emanuel *(1949-)* Polish-born American pianist.

Bb

Babbitt, Milton *(1916-)* American composer and theoretician.

Bach, Carl Phillipp Emanuel *(1714-1788)* German composer.

Bach, Johann Christian *(1735-1782)* German composer.

Bach, Johann Christoph *(1642-1703)* German composer.

Bach, Johann Christoph Friedrich *(1732-1795)* German composer.

Bach, Johann Sebastian *(1685-1750)* German composer-organist.

Bach, Wilhelm Friedemann *(1710-1784)* German composer.

Bacharach, Burt *(1928-)* American composer of shows and films.

Bacon, Ernst *(1898-1990)* American composer.

Baez, Joan *(1941-)* American folk singer.

Baker, David *(1931-)* American jazz composer-author-pedagogue.

Balakirev, Mily *(1837-1910)* Russian composer.

Barber, Samuel *(1910-1981)* American composer.

Barlow, Wayne *(1912-)* American composer.

Bartok, Bela *(1881-1945)* Hungarian composer.

Basie, William "Count" *(1906-1984)* American jazz pianist and bandleader.

Bassett, Leslie *(1923-)* American composer.

Bauer, Marion *(1887-1955)* American composer-pedagogue.

Bechet, Sidney *(1897-1959)* American jazz clarinetist-saxophonist.

Beecham, Sir Thomas *(1879-1961)* English conductor.

Beeson, Jack *(1921-)* American opera composer.

Beethoven, Ludwig van *(1770-1827)* German composer.

Beiderbecke, Bix *(1903-1931)* American jazz cornetist.

Belafonte, Harry *(1927-)* American singer-actor.

Bellini, Vincenzo *(1801-1835)* Italian opera composer.

Bennett, Robert Russell *(1894-1981)* American composer-arranger.

Benson, Warren *(1924-)* American composer.

Benzanson, Philip *(1916-)* American composer.

Berg, Alban *(1885-1935)* Austrian twelve-tone composer.

Bergsma, William *(1921-)* American composer.

Berio, Luciano *(1925-)* Italian composer.

Berlin, Irving *(1888-1989)* American composer of shows and popular music.

Berlioz, Hector *(1803-1869)* French orchestral composer.

Bernstein, Leonard *(1918-1990)* American conductor-composer-pianist.

Berry, Chuck *(1926-)* American singer-guitarist-songwriter.

Bigard, Barney *(1906-1980)* American jazz clarinetist.

Billings, William *(1746-1800)* American composer.

Bing, Sir Rudolf *(1902-)* Austrian-born opera impresario; former general manager of the Metropolitan Opera.

Bizet, Georges *(1838-1875)* French opera composer.

Blackwood, Easley *(1933-)* American composer.

Blake, James Hubert "Eubie" *(1883-1983)* American ragtime pianist-composer.

Blech, Leo *(1871-1958)* German composer.

Bley, Paul *(1932-)* American jazz keyboard performer.

Bloch, Ernest *(1880-1959)* Swiss-born American composer.

Block, Ray *(1902-1982)* American conductor.

Blow, John *(1649-1708)* English organist-composer.

Boccherini, Luigi *(1743-1805)* Italian chamber music composer.

Balcom, William *(1938-)* American composer-ragtime pianist.

Bolden, Charles "Buddy" *(1870-1931)* American jazz cornetist.

Borodin, Alexander *(1833-1887)* Russian opera composer.

Boulanger, Lili *(1893-1918)* French composer.

Boulanger, Nadia *(1887-1979)* French pedagogue-composer-conductor.

Boulez, Pierre *(1925-)* French composer-conductor.

Braff, Ruby *(1927-)* American jazz trumpet player.

Brahms, Johannes *(1833-1897)* German composer.

Britten, Benjamin *(1913-1976)* English opera composer.

Brown, Earle *(1926-)* American composer.

Brown, James *(1928-)* American soul singer.

Brubeck, Dave *(1920-)* American jazz pianist-composer.

Bruch, Max *(1838-1920)* German composer.

Bruckner, Anton *(1824-1896)* Austrian symphonic composer.

Burgmuller, Friedrich, Johann Franz *(1806-1874)* French composer.

Burke, Johnny *(1908-1964)* American popular composer.

Burns, Ralph *(1922-)* American songwriter-arranger.

Burrell, Kenny *(1931-)* American jazz guitarist.

Busoni, Ferruccio *(1866-1924)* Italian-German composer-pianist- author.

Buxtehude, Dietrich *(1637-1707)* German organist-composer.

Byrd, Donald *(1932-)* American composer-jazz trumpet player-pedagogue.

Byrd, William *(1543-1623)* English organist-vocal composer.

Cc

Caccini, Giulio *(1550-1618)* Italian opera composer.

Cage, John *(1912-1992)* American composer.

Carissimi, Giacomo *(1605-1674)* Italian oratorio composer.

Carmichael, Hoagland "Hoagy" *(1899-1981)* American songwriter pianist.

Carpenter, Karen A. *(1950-1983)* American pop singer.

Carter, Benny *(1907-)* American jazz saxophonist-composer, arranger.

Carter, Elliott *(1908-)* American composer.

Casadesus, Robert *(1899-1972)* French pianist-composer.

Casals, Pablo *(1876-1973)* Spanish cellist.

Casella, Alfredo *(1883-1947)* Italian composer pianist.

Cash, Johnny *(1932-)* American country singer-guitarist songwriter.

Chaminade, Cecile *(1857-1944)* French composer of piano salon music.

Charles, Ray *(1930-)* American pop singer-composer.

Chavez, Carlos *(1899-1978)* Mexican composer.

Checker, Chubby (Ernest Evans) *(1941-)* American rock 'n' roll singer.

Cherubini, Luigi *(1760-1842)* Italian opera composer.

Chihara, Paul *(1938-)* American composer.

Childs, Barney *(1926-)* American composer.

Chopin, Frederic *(1810-1849)* Polish pianist-composer.

Chou, Wen-chung *(1923-)* Chinese-American composer.

Christian, Charlie *(1919-1942)* American jazz guitarist.

Cimarosa, Domenico *(1749-1801)* Italian opera composer.

Clarke, Jeremiah *(1673-1707)* English composer.

Clarke, Kenny "Klook" *(1914-1985)* American jazz drummer.

Clementi, Muzio *(1752-1832)* Italian pianist-composer-pedagogue.

Cliburn, Van *(1934-)* American pianist.

Cole, Nat "King" *(1917-1965)* American jazz pianist-singer.

Cole, William R. "Cozy" *(1909-1981)* American jazz drummer.

Coleman, Cy *(1929-)* Popular-theatre songwriter.

Coleman, Ornette *(1930-)* American jazz saxophonist-composer.

Colgrass, Michael *(1932-)* American composer.

Coltrane, John *(1926-1967)* American jazz saxophonist-composer.

Condon, Eddie *(1904-)* American jazz guitarist.

Cook, Will Marion *(1869-1944)* American composer of black musical comedies.

Copland, Aaron *(1900-1990)* American composer.

Corelli, Arcangelo *(1653-1713)* Italian violinist-composer.

Corigliano, John *(1938-)* American composer.

Coslow, Sam *(1910-1982)* American songwriter-lyricist.

Couperin, Francois *(1668-1733)* French keyboard composer-organist.

Cowell, Henry *(1897-1965)* American composer.

Craft, Robert *(1923-)* American conductor-writer

Creston, Paul *(1906-1985)* American composer.

Crosby, Bing (Harry Lillis Crosby) *(1901-1977)* American pop singer actor.

Cruger, Johann *(1598-1662)* German pedagogue.

Crumb, George *(1929-)* American composer.

Cui, Cesar *(1835-1918)* Russian composer.

Czerny, Carl *(1791-1857)* Austrian composer-pianist.

Dd

Dahl, Ingolf *(1912-1970)* American composer-pedagogue.

Dallapiccola, Luigi *(1904-1975)* Italian composer.

Damrosch, Walter *(1862-1950)* German-American conductor-composer.

Davidovsky, Mario *(1934-)* Argentinian-American composer.

Davies, Peter Maxwell *(1934-)* English composer.

Davis, Miles *(1926-1991)* American jazz trumpet player-composer.

Davis, Sammy, Jr. *(1925-1990)* American pop singer-dancer-actor.

Debussy, Claude *(1862-1918)* French composer.

Delibes, Leo *(1836-1891)* French composer of ballets and operas.

Delius, Frederick *(1862-1934)* English composer.

Dello Joio, Norman *(1913-)* American composer.

Del Tredici, David *(1937-)* American composer.

Desmond Paul (Paul Emil Breitenfeld) *(1924-1977)* American jazz alto saxophone player.

Des Prez, Josquin *(1440-1521)* Flemish polyphonic composer.

Diabelli, Anton *(1781-1858)* Austrian composer-publisher.

Diamond, David *(1915-)* American composer.

Dichter, Misha *(1945-)* Russian-American pianist.

Dittersdorf, Karl Ditters von *(1739-1799)* Austrian violinist- composer.

Domino, Antoine "Fats" *(1928-)* American rock 'n' roll singer-pianist-songwriter.

Donato, Anthony *(1909-)* American composer.

Donizetti, Gaetano *(1797-1848)* Italian opera composer.

Dorati, Antal *(1906-)* Hungarian-American conductor.

Dorsey, Jimmy *(1904-1957)* American bandleader-jazz woodwind player.

Dorsey, Tommy *(1905-1956)* American bandleader-trombonist.

Dowland, John *(1562-1626)* English composer-lutenist.

Dragon, Carmen *(1914-1984)* American composer-conductor.

Druckman, Jacob *(1928-)* American composer.

Dufay, Guillaume *(1400-1474)* Flemish composer.

Dukas, Paul *(1865-1935)* French composer.

Duke, Vernon (Vladimir Dukelsky) *(1903-1969)* Russian-American composer-songwriter.

Dunstable, John *(1380-1453)* English composer.

Dupre, Marcel *(1886-1971)* French organist.

Dussek, Jan Ladislav *(1760-1812)* Czech pianist-composer.

Dvorak, Antonin *(1841-1904)* Czech composer.

Dylan, Bob (Robert Zimmerman) *(1941-)* American folk-rock-songwriter-singer.

Ee

Eccles, John *(1668-1735)* English composer.

Eckstine, Billy *(1914-)* American jazz singer.

Edison, Thomas Alva *(1847-1931)* American inventor of the phonograph.

Effinger, Cecil *(1914-1990)* American composer.

El-Daph, Halim *(1921-)* Egyptian composer.

Elgar, Sir Edward *(1857-1934)* English composer.

Ellington, Edward Kennedy "Duke" *(1899-1974)* American composer-jazz pianist-bandleader.

Enesco, Georges *(1881-1955)* Russian violinist-composer.

Erb, Donald *(1927-)* American composer.

Escobar, Luis Antonio *(1925-)* Colombian composer.

Etler, Alvin *(1913-1973)* American composer.

Evans, Bill *(1919-1980)* American jazz pianist-composer.

Evans, Gil *(1912-1988)* Canadian-American jazz arranger-composer.

Ewen, David *(1907-1985)* American writer-musicologist.

Ff

Falla, Manuel de *(1816-1946)* Spanish composer.

Farrell, Eileen *(1920-)* American operatic-concert soprano.

Faure, Gabriel *(1845-1924)* French composer-pedagogue.

Feldman, Morton *(1926-1987)* American composer.

Ferguson, Maynard *(1928-)* Canadian-American trumpeter-bandleader.

Fiedler, Arthur *(1894-1979)* American conductor of the Boston Pops Orchestra.

Fine, Irving *(1914-1962)* American composer.

Finney, Ross Lee *(1906-)* American composer.

Fitzgerald, Ella *(1918-)* American jazz singer.

Flagello, Nicholas *(1928-)* American composer.

Floyd, Carlisle *(1926-)* American opera composer.

Foss, Lukas *(1922-)* German-American pianist-composer-conductor.

Foster, Stephen *(1826-1864)* American popular song composer.

Fox, Virgil *(1912-1980)* American organist.

Franck, Cesar *(1822-1890)* French organist-composer.

Franklin, Aretha *(1942-)* American soul singer.

Frescobaldi, Girolamo *(1583-1643)* Italian organist-composer.

Friml, Rudolf *(1881-1972)* Czech-American operetta composer.

Gg

Gabrieli, Andrea *(1520-1586)* Italian organist-composer.

Gabrieli, Giovanni *(1557-1612)* Italian organist-composer.

Gaburo, Kenneth *(1926-)* American composer.

Ganz, Rudolph *(1877-1972)* Swiss-American composer.

Garfunkel, Art *(1941-)* American folk singer.

Garland, Judy *(1922-1969)* American singer-actress.

Garner, Erroll *(1923-1977)* American jazz pianist-composer.

Gershwin, George *(1898-1937)* American songwriter-composer.

Gershwin, Ira *(1896-1983)* American lyricist-librettist.

Getz, Stan *(1927-1991)* American jazz tenor saxophonist.

Giannini, Vittorio *(1903-1966)* American composer.

Gibbons, Orlando *(1583-1625)* English composer.

Gideon, Miriam *(1906-)* American composer.

Gillespie, John Birks "Dizzy" *(1917-1993)* American jazz trumpet player-composer-arranger.

Gillis, Don *(1912-1978)* American composer.

Gillmore, Patrick *(1829-1892)* American bandmaster.

Ginastera, Alberto *(1916-1983)* Argentinian composer.

Glass, Philip *(1937-)* American composer.

Glazunov, Alexander *(1865-1936)* Russian composer-pedagogue.

Gliere, Reinhold *(1875-1956)* Russian composer-pedagogue.

Glinka, Mikhail *(1804-1857)* Russian composer.

Gluck, Christoph Willibald von *(1714-1787)* German opera composer.

Godowsky, Leopold *(1870-1938)* Russian-American pianist-composer.

Goldman, Edwin Franko *(1878-1956)* American bandmaster.

Goldman, Richard Franko *(1910-1980)* American bandmaster.

Goldmark, Rubin *(1872-1936)* American composer-pedagogue.

Goodman, Benny *(1909-1986)* American jazz clarinetist-bandleader.

Goosens, Sir Eugene *(1893-1962)* English conductor-composer.

Gossec, Francois Joseph *(1734-1829)* Belgian composer.

Gottschalk, Louis Moreau *(1829-1869)* American pianist-composer.

Gould, Glenn *(1932-1982)* Canadian pianist.

Gould, Morton *(1913-)* American composer-conductor.

Gounod, Charles *(1818-1893)* French opera composer.

Grainger, Percy *(1882-1961)* Australian pianist-composer.

Grappelli, Stephane *(1908-)* French jazz violinist.

Greer, William A. "Sonny" *(1903-1982)* American jazz big band drummer.

Grieg, Edvard *(1843-1907)* Norwegian composer.

Griffes, Charles Tomlinson *(1884-1920)* American composer.

Grofe, Ferde *(1892-1972)* American composer-arranger.

Guilmant, Alexandre *(1837-1911)* French organist.

Gurlitt, Cornelius *(1820-1901)* German composer.

Guthrie, Woody *(1912-1967)* American folk singer-guitarist-songwriter.

Hh

Haley, Bill *(1927-1981)* American rock'n'roll singer.

Hames, Dick *(1914-1980)* American pop singer.

Hammerstein, Oscar, II *(1895-1960)* American lyricist-librettist.

Hampton, Lionel *(1913-)* American jazz vibraphonist-bandleader.

Hancock, Herbie *(1940-)* American jazz keyboardist-composer.

Handel, George Frideric *(1685-1759)* German organist-composer.

Handy, W.C. *(1873-1958)* American songwriter.

Hanon, Charles-Louis *(1819-1900)* French pianist-pedagogue-composer.

Hanson, Howard *(1896-1981)* American composer-pedagogue.

Harris, Roy *(1898-1979)* American composer.

Harrison, George *(1943-)* English rock singer-guitarist - songwriter - Beatle.

Harrison, Lou *(1917-)* American composer.

Hart, Lorenz *(1895-1941)* American lyricist.

Hassler, Hans Leo *(1564-1612)* German composer.

Hawkins, Coleman *(1904-1969)* American jazz tenor saxophonist.

Haydn, Franz Joseph *(1732-1809)* Austrian composer.

Haydn, Michael *(1737-1806)* Austrian composer.

Heiden, Bernhard *(1910-)* German-American composer-pedagogue.

Heifetz, Jascha *(1901-1987)* Russian-American violinist.

Henderson, Fletcher *(1898-1952)* American jazz pianist-arranger-band-leader.

Henderson, Skitch *(1918-)* American pianist-bandleader.

Henze, Hans Werner *(1926-)* German composer.

Herbert, Victor *(1859-1924)* American operetta composer.

Herman, Woody *(1913-1987)* American jazz clarinetist-bandleader.

Herrmann, Bernard *(1911-1975)* American movie composer.

Herz, Henri *(1803-1888)* Austrian pianist-composer.

Hiller, Lejaren *(1924-)* American computer music composer.

Hindemith, Paul *(1895-1963)* German composer.

Hines, Earl "Fatha" *(1905-1983)* American jazz pianist-bandleader.

Hirt, Al *(1922-)* American jazz trumpet player.

Hodkinson, Sydney *(1934-)* Canadian composer.

Holiday, Billie *(1915-1959)* American jazz vocalist.

Hollander, Lorin *(1944-)* American pianist.

Holst, Gustav *(1874-1934)* English composer.

Honegger, Arthur *(1892-1955)* French composer.

Hooker, John Lee *(1917-)* American blues singer-guitarist.

Horne, Marilyn *(1934-)* American operatic soprano.

Horowitz, Vladimir *(1903-1989)* Russian-American pianist.

Hovhaness, Alan *(1911-)* American composer.

Hubbard, Freddie *(1938-)* American jazz trumpet player.

Humes, Helen *(1913-1981)* American jazz singer.

Hummel, Johann Nepomuk *(1778-1837)* Czech pianist-composer.

Humperdinck, Engelbert *(1854-1921)* German composer.

Hunt, Walter "Pee Wee" *(1907-1979)* American jazz trombone player.

Husa, Karel *(1921-)* Czech-American composer.

Ii

Ibert, Jacques *(1890-1962)* French composer.

Ireland, John *(1879-1962)* English composer.

Iturbi, Jose *(1895-1980)* Spanish-American pianist-conductor.

Ives, Burl *(1909-)* American folk singer-actor.

Ives, Charles Edward *(1874-1954)* American composer.

Jj

Jackson, Milt *(1923-)* American jazz vibraphone player.

Jacob, Gordon *(1895-1984)* English composer.

James, Harry *(1916-1983)* American trumpet player-bandleader.

Janacek, Leos *(1854-1928)* Czech composer.

Jarnach, Philipp *(1892-1982)* Spanish composer.

Jenkins, Gordon *(1910-1984)* American composer-conductor.

Johnson, James P. *(1891-1955)* American jazz pianist-composer.

Johnson, Thor *(1913-1975)* American conductor.

Johnson, William "Bunk" *(1879-1949)* American jazz trumpet player.

Johnston, Ben *(1926-)* American composer.

Jolson, Al *(1886-1950)* American popular minstrel singer

Jones, Hank *(1918-)* American jazz pianist.

Jones, Jo *(1912-1985)* American jazz drummer.

Jones, "Philly" Joe *(1923-1985)* American jazz drummer.

Jones, Quincy *(1933-)* American jazz trumpet player-composer-arranger-producer.

Jones, Thad *(1923-1986)* American jazz trumpet player-composer-bandleader.

Jones, Tom *(1940-)* Welsh pop singer.

Joplin, Janis *(1943-1970)* American rock singer.

Joplin, Scott *(1868-1917)* American ragtime pianist-composer.

Juilliard, Augustus D. *(1836-1919)* French-American music patron and founder of the Juilliard School of Music.

Kk

Kabalevsky, Dmitri *(1904-1987)* Russian composer.

Kagel, Mauricio *(1931-)* Argentinian composer.

Kay, Ulysses *(1917-)* American composer.

Kennan, Kent Wheeler *(1913-)* American composer-pedagogue.

Kenton, Stan *(1911-1979)* American bandleader, pianist-composer-arranger.

Kern, Jerome *(1885-1945)* American musical comedy composer.

Khachaturian, Aram *(1903-1978)* Russian-Armenian composer.

King, B. B. *(1925-)* American blues singer-guitarist-songwriter.

King, Wayne *(1901-1985)* American pop bandleader.

Kinkeldey, Otto *(1818-1966)* American musicologist.

Kirchner, Leon *(1919-)* American composer.

Kirk, Rahsaan Roland *(1936-1977)* American jazz woodwind player.

Kirkpatrick, Ralph *(1911-)* American harpsichordist- musicologist.

Klemperer, Otto *(1885-1973)* German conductor.

Klose, Hyacinthe-Eleonore *(1808-1880)* French clarinetist-pedagogue.

Kodaly, Zoltan *(1882-1967)* Hungarian composer-pedagogue.

Kohler, Louis *(1820-1886)* German pianist-pedagogue.

Korngold, Erich Wolfgang *(1897-1957)* Austrian-American composer.

Kostelanetz, Andre *(1901-1980)* Russian-American conductor.

Koussevitzky, Serge *(1874-1951)* Russian conductor-double bassist.

Kraft, William *(1923-)* American composer-percussionist.

Krebs, Johann Ludwig *(1713-1780)* German composer-organist.

Kreisler, Fritz *(1875-1962)* Austrian violinist-composer.

Krenek, Ernest *(1900-1991)* Austrian-American composer.

Kristofferson, Kris *(1937-)* American country singer-actor- songwriter.

Krupa, Gene *(1909-1973)* American jazz drummer-bandleader.

Kubik, Gail *(1914-1984)* American composer.

Kuhlau, Friedrich *(1786-1832)* German composer.

Kuhnau, Johann *(1660-1722)* German composer.

Kyser, Kay *(1906-1985)* American pop bandleader.

Ll

Landerman, Ezra *(1924-)* American composer.

Lalo, Edouard *(1823-1892)* French composer.

Landowska, Wanda *(1877-1959)* Polish harpsichordist.

Lane, Burton (Morris Hyman Kushner) *(1912-)* American Broadway musical composer.

Langlais, Jean *(1907-1991)* French composer.

Lanza, Alcides *(1929-)* Argentinian composer.

Lassus, Orlande de *(1532-1594)* Dutch composer.

Lateef, Yusef *(1921-)* American jazz woodwind player-composer.

Leadbelly (Huddie Ledbetter) *(1885-1949)* American folk singer-guitarist-songwriter.

Lee, Dai-Keong *(1915-)* American composer.

Lee, Peggy *(1920-)* American popular jazz-singer.

Legrand, Michel *(1932-)* French pianist-composer.

Lehar, Franz *(1870-1948)* Austrian operetta composer.

Leighton, Kenneth (1929-) English composer.

Leinsdorf, Erich *(1912-)* Austrian conductor.

Lennon, John *(1940-1980)* English rock singer-guitarist-songwriter-Beatle.

Leoncavallo, Ruggiero *(1857-1919)* Italian opera composer.

Levant, Oscar *(1906-1967)* American pianist-composer-actor.

Lewis, Henry *(1932-)* American conductor.

Lewis, Jerry Lee *(1935-)* American rock'n'roll singer-pianist.

Lewis, John *(1920-)* American jazz pianist-composer.

Lewis, Mel *(1929-1989)* American jazz drummer-bandleader.

Liberace (Wladziu, Valentino) *(1919-1987)* American pop pianist.

Lieberson, Goddard *(1911-1977)* American composer-recording executive.

List, Eugene *(1918-1985)* American pianist-pedagogue.

Liszt, Franz *(1811-1886)* Hungarian pianist-composer.

Little, Richard (Richard Penniman) *(1935-)* American rock'n'roll singer-songwriter.

Lockwood, Normand *(1906-)* American composer.

Loesser, Arthur *(1894-1969)* American pianist-author.

Loesser, Frank *(1910-1969)* American Broadway musical composer.

Loewe, Frederick *(1904-1986)* Austrian-American Broadway musical composer.

Luening, Otto *(1900-)* American composer.

Lully, Jean-Baptiste *(1632-1687)* Italian composer.

Luther, Martin *(1483-1546)* German hymnologist-religious reformer.

Lutoslawski, Witold *(1913-)* Polish composer.

Mm

Maazel, Lorin *(1930-)* American conductor.

MacDowell, Edward Alexander *(1860-1908)* American composer.

Machaut, Guillaume de *(1300-1377)* Polyphonic composer.

Mahler, Gustav *(1860-1911)* Austrian composer-conductor.

Mancini, Henry *(1924-)* American television-film composer.

Manne, Shelly *(1920-1984)* American jazz drummer-composer.

Markevitch, Igor *(1912-1983)* Russian-French composer-conductor.

Marks, Gerald *(1900-)* American songwriter-lyricist.

Marks, Johnny *(1909-1985)* American songwriter.

Martin, Frank *(1890-1974)* Swiss composer.

Martin, Freddie *(1906-1983)* American bandleader.

Martin, Mary *(1913-1990)* American Broadway musical soprano.

Mascagni, Pietro *(1863-1945)* Italian opera composer.

Mason, Lowell *(1792-1872)* American organist-pedagogue.

Massenet, Jules *(1842-1912)* French opera composer.

Mayuzumi, Toshiro *(1929-)* Japanese composer.

McCartney, Paul *(1942-)* English rock singer-bassist-songwriter-Beatle.

McPartland, Jimmie *(1907-1991)* American jazz cornetist.

McPartland, Marian *(1920-)* English-American jazz pianist.

Mehegan, John *(1920-)* American jazz pianist-writer-pedagogue.

Mehta, Zubin *(1936-)* Indian-American conductor.

Mendelssohn, Felix *(1809-1847)* German composer.

Mendes, Sergio *(1941-)* Brazilian pop pianist-composer-bandleader.

Mennin, Peter *(1923-1983)* American composer-pedagogue.

Menotti, Gian Carlo *(1911-)* Italian-American opera composer.

Menuhin, Yehudi *(1916-)* American violinist.

Merman, Ethel *(1909-1984)* American Broadway musical singer-actress.

Messiaen, Olivier *(1908-1992)* French composer.

Mester, Jorge *(1935-)* Mexican-American conductor.

Meyerbeer, Giacomo *(1791-1864)* German-French opera composer.

Milhaud, Darius *(1892-1974)* French-American composer-pedagogue.

Miller, Glenn *(1904-1944)* American bandleader-trombonist.

Mingus, Charles *(1922-1979)* American jazz bass player-composer.

Mitchell, Richard A. "Blue" *(1930-1979)* American jazz trumpet player.

Monk, Thelonious *(1918-1982)* American jazz pianist-composer.

Monteux, Pierre *(1875-1964)* French conductor.

Monteverdi, Claudio *(1567-1643)* Italian opera composer.

Moog, Robert A. *(1934-)* American inventor of the Moog synthesizer.

Moore, Douglas *(1893-1969)* American composer.

Morley, Thomas *(1557-1602)* English madrigal composer.

Morton, Jelly Roll (Ferdinand Joseph La Menthe) (1885-1941) American jazz pianist-composer-arranger.

Mozart, Leopold *(1719-1787)* Austrian violinist-composer.

Mozart, Wolfgang Amadeus *(1756-1791)* Austrian pianist-composer.

Mulligan, Gerry *(1927-)* American jazz bariton saxophone player-composer-arranger-bandleader.

Munch, Charles *(1891-1968)* Alsatian conductor.

Mussorgsky, Modest *(1839-1881)* Russian opera composer.

Nn

Nabokov, Nicolas *(1903-1978)* Russian-American composer.

Nelhybel, Vaclav *(1919-)* Czech composer.

Nelson, Ron J. *(1929-)* American composer-pedagogue.

Newman, Alfred *(1900-1970)* American film composer.

Nicolai, Otto *(1810-1861)* German opera composer.

Nielsen, Carl *(1865-1931)* Danish composer.

Nilsson, Birgit *(1918-)* Swedish Wagnerian soprano.

Nilsson, Bo *(1937-)* Swedish composer.

Nono, Luigi *(1924- 1990)* Italian composer.

Nordoff, Paul *(1909-1977)* American composer.

Oo

Obrecht, Jacob (1450-1505) Flemish church composer.

Offenbach, Jacques *(1819-1880)* French operetta composer.

Oliver, Joe "King" *(1885-1938)* American New Orleans jazz cornet player.

Oliver, Sy *(1910-1988)* American jazz trumpet player-arranger.

Orff, Carl *(1895-1982)* German composer-pedagogue.

Ormandy, Eugene *(1899-1985)* Hungarian-American conductor.

Ornstein, Leo *(1892-)* Russian-American pianist-composer.

Ory, Kid *(1886-1973)* American jazz trombone player.

Overton, Hall *(1920-1972)* American composer-jazz pianist.

Ozawa, Seiji *(1935-)* Japanese-American conductor.

Pp

Pachelbel, Carl Theodorus *(1690-1750)* German-American organist-composer.

Paderewski, Ignace *(1860-1941)* Polish pianist-composer.

Paganini, Niccolo *(1782-1840)* Italian violinist-composer.

Palestrina, Giovanni Pierluigi da *(1525-1594)* Italian choral composer.

Parker, Charlie "Bird" *(1920-1955)* American alto saxophone player-composer.

Parker, Horatio *(1863-1918)* American composer-pedagogue.

Partch, Harry *(1901-1974)* American composer-instrument inventor.

Parton, Dolly *(1946-)* American country music singer-songwriter.

Peerce, Jan *(1904-1984)* American opera tenor.

Peeters, Flor *(1903-1986)* Belgian organist-composer.

Penderecki, Krzysztof *(1933-)* Polish composer.

Pepusch, Johann Christoph *(1667-1752)* German-English composer-arranger.

Pergolesi, Giovanni Battista *(1710-1736)* Italian opera buffa composer.

Peri, Jacopo *(1561-1633)* Italian opera composer.

Perle, George *(1915-)* American composer.

Persichetti, Vincent *(1915-1987)* American composer-pedagogue.

Peters, Roberta *(1930-)* American operatic soprano.

Peterson, Oscar *(1925-)* Canadian jazz pianist.

Petrillo, James C. *(1892-1984)* American trumpeter-president of the American Federation of Musicians.

Phillips, Burrill *(1907-1988)* American composer.

Piatigorsky, Gregor (1903-1976) Russian cellist.

Piston, Walter *(1894-1976)* American composer-author-pedagogue.

Porter, Cole *(1891-1964)* American musical theatre composer-lyricist.

Porter, Quincy *(1897-1966)* American composer.

Poulenc, Francis *(1899-1963)* French composer.

Powell, Earl "Bud" *(1924-1966)* American jazz pianist-composer.

Powell, Mel *(1923-)* American composer-pedagogue.

Praetorius, Michael *(1571-1621)* German organist-theorist.

Presley, Elvis *(1935-1977)* American rock'n'roll singer-actor.

Previn, Andre *(1929-)* German-American conductor-composer-jazz pianist.

Price, Leontyne *(1927-)* American operatic soprano.

Prima, Louis *(1910-1978)* American jazz-pop trumpet player-singer-bandleader.

Primrose, William *(1903-1982)* Scottish violinist-pedagogue.

Prokofiev, Sergei *(1891-1953)* Russian composer.

Pryor, Arthur *(1870-1942)* American trombonist-composer-band director.

Puccini, Giacomo *(1858-1924)* Italian opera composer.

Purcell, Henry *(1659-1695)* English composer.

Qq

Quantz, Johann Joachim *(1697-1773)* German Flute player-composer theorist.

Quintanar, Hector *(1936-)* Mexican composer.

Rr

Rachmaninoff, Sergei *(1873-1943)* Russian pianist-composer.

Rainey, Gertrude "Ma" *(1886-1939)* American blues singer.

Rameau, Jean-Philippe *(1683-1764)* French composer-theorist.

Ravel, Maurice *(1875-1937)* French composer.

Read, Daniel *(1757-1836)* American composer-voice pedagogue.

Read, Gardner *(1913-)* American composer-author.

Reed, Herbert Owen *(1910-)* American composer-pedagogue.

Reese, Gustave *(1899-1977)* American musicologist.

Reger, Max *(1873-1916)* German composer-organist-pedagogue.

Reich, Steve *(1936-)* American composer.

Reinecke, Carl *(1824-1910)* German pianist-composer-conductor.

Reiner, Fritz *(1888-1963)* Hungarian-American conductor.

Reinhardt, Django *(1910-1953)* Belgian jazz guitarist.

Respighi, Ottorino *(1879-1936)* Italian composer.

Reubke, Julius *(1834-1858)* German composer-organist.

Reynolds, Roger *(1934-)* American composer.

Ricci, Ruggiero *(1918-)* American violinist.

Rich, Buddy *(1917-1987)* American jazz drummer-bandleader.

Richter, Hans *(1843-1916)* Hungarian-German conductor.

Riegger, Wallingford *(1885-1961)* American composer.

Rimsky-Korsakov, Nikolai *(1844-1908)* Russian composer.

Ritter, Tex *(1905-1974)* American country and western singer-guitarist-actor.

Roach, Max *(1925-   )* American jazz drummer.

Robeson, Paul *(1898-1976)* American bass singer-actor.

Rochberg, George *(1918-   )* American composer.

Rodgers, Richard *(1902-1979)* American musical theatre composer-songwriter.

Rogers, Bernard *(1893-1968)* American composer-pedagogue.

Rogers, Roy *(1912-   )* American singer-actor cowboy.

Ronstadt, Linda *(1943-   )* American pop singer.

Rorem, Ned *(1923-   )* American song composer.

Rose, Leonard *(1918-   )* American cellist.

Ross, Diana *(1944-   )* American pop-soul singer.

Rossini, Gioacchino *(1792-1868)* Italian opera composer.

Rousseau, Jean-Jacques *(1712-1778)* French opera composer-philosopher.

Rubinstein, Anton *(1829-1894)* Russian pianist-composer.

Rubinstein, Arthur *(1886-1982)* Polish pianist.

Rudel, Julius *(1921-   )* Viennese-American opera conductor.

Ruggles, Carl *(1876-1971)* American composer-pedagogue.

Ss

Saint-Saens, Camille *(1835-1921)* French composer.

Salieri, Antonio *(1750-1825)* Italian opera and church music composer.

Salzedo, Carlos *(1885-1961)* French-American harpist-composer-author.

Salzman, Eric *(1933-)* American composer.

Sanders, Pharoah *(1940-)* American jazz saxophone player.

Satie, Erik *(1866-1925)* French composer.

Sax, Adolphe *(1814-1894)* Belgian saxophone inventor.

Scarlatti, Alessandro *(1660-1725)* Italian opera composer.

Scarlatti, Domenico *(1685-1757)* Italian harpsichord composer.

Scheidt, Samuel *(1587-1654)* German organist-composer.

Schein, Johann Hermann *(1586-1630)* German church music composer.

Scherchen, Hermann *(1891-1966)* German conductor.

Schickele, Peter *(1935-)* American composer-musical humorist.

Schifrin, Lalo *(1932-)* Argentinian-American pianist-jazz musician-film composer.

Schillinger, Joseph *(1895-1943)* Russian-American composer-author.

Schippers, Thomas *(1930-1977)* American conductor.

Schnabel, Artur *(1882-1951)* Austrian pianist-pedagogue.

Schoenberg, Arnold *(1874-1951)* Austrian composer-twelve-tone music originator.

Schubert, Franz *(1797-1828)* Austrian composer.

Schuller, Gunther *(1925-)* American composer-conductor-horn player-pedagogue.

Schuman, William *(1910-)* American composer-pedagogue.

Schumann, Clara *(1819-1896)* German pianist-composer.

Schumann, Robert *(1810-1856)* German composer-author.

Schutz, Heinrich *(1585-1672)* German composer.

Schwartz, Arthur *(1900-1984)* American Broadway show composer.

Scott, James Sylvester *(1886-1938)* American ragtime pianist-composer.

Scriabin, Alexander *(1872-1915)* Russian composer.

Seeger, Pete *(1919-)* American folk singer-composer.

Segovia, Andres *(1893-1987)* Spanish guitarist.

Serebrier, Jose *(1938-)* Uruguayan conductor-composer.

Serkin, Peter *(1947-)* American pianist.

Sessions, Roger *(1896-1985)* American composer.

Severinsen, Carl "Doc" *(1927-)* American trumpet player- bandleader.

Shank, Bud *(1926-)* American jazz woodwind player.   '

Shankar, Ravi *(1920-)* Indian composer-sitarist.

Shapey, Ralph *(1921-)* American conductor-composer.

Shaw, Artie *(1910-)* American clarinet player-bandleader.

Shaw, Robert *(1916-)* American conductor.

Shearing, George *(1919-)* English-American jazz pianist-composer.

Shepp, Archie *(1937-)* American jazz saxophonist.

Shostakovich, Dmitri *(1906-1975)* Russian composer.

Sibelius, Jean *(1865-1957)* Finnish composer.

Siegmeister, Elie *(1909-1991)* American composer.

Sills, Beverly *(1929-)* American operatic soprano.

Silver, Horace *(1926-)* American jazz pianist-composer.

Simon, Paul *(1941-)* American folk-rock singer-songwriter.

Sims, "Zoot" John Haley *(1925-1985)* American jazz tenor saxophone player.

Sinatra, Frank *(1915-)* American pop singer-actor.

Skrowaczewski, Stanislaw *(1923-)* Polish conductor-composer.

Slonimsky, Nicolas *(1894-)* Russian-American pianist-conductor-composer-lexicographer.

Smetana, Bedrich *(1824-1884)* Bohemian composer.

Smith, Bessie *(1895-1937)* American blues singer.

Smith, Clarence "Pinetop" *(1904-1929)* American boogie-woogie pianist-blues singer.

Smith, Hale *(1925-)* American composer-pedagogue.

Smith, Kate *(1909-1986)* American pop singer.

Smith, Willie "The Lion" *(1897-1973)* American stride pianist.

Solti, Sir George *(1912-)* British-American conductor.

Sondheim, Stephen *(1930-)* American Broadway musical composer-lyricist.

Sousa, John Philip *(1854-1932)* American bandmaster-composer.

Sowerby, Leo *(1895-1968)* American composer.

Spanier, Frances "Muggsy" *(1906-1967)* American jazz cornet player.

Spector, Phil *(1940-)* American songwriter-record producer.

Spitalny, Phil *(1890-1970)* Russian-American bandleader.

Spivak, Charlie *(1905-1982)* American bandleader-trumpet player.

Spohr, Ludwig *(1784-1859)* German violinist-conductor-composer.

Stamitz, Carl *(1745-1801)* Bohemian violinist-composer.

Stamitz, Johann (1717-1757) Bohemian composer.

Starer, Robert *(1924-)* American composer.

Starker, Janos *(1924-)* Hungarian-American cellist.

Starr, Ringo (Richard Starkey) *(1940-)* English rock drummer-Beatle

Stern, Isaac *(1920-)* American violinist.

Stevens, Halsey *(1908-)* American composer-pedagogue.

Stevens, Rise *(1913-)* American opera-pop mezzo-soprano.

Stewart, Slam *(1914-1988)* American jazz bass player.

Still, William Grant *(1895-1978)* American composer.

Stitt, Sonny *(1924-1982)* American jazz saxophone player.

Stockhausen, Karlheinz *(1928-)* German composer.

Stokowski, Leopold *(1882-1977)* English-American conductor.

Strang, Gerald *(1908-)* American composer.

Strauss, Johann, Jr. *(1825-1899)* Austrian composer.

Strauss, Richard *(1864-1949)* German composer.

Stravinsky, Igor *(1882-1971)* Russian-American composer.

Strayhorn, Billy *(1915-1967)* American jazz composer-arranger.

Streisand, Barbra *(1942-)* American pop singer-actress.

Styne, Jule *(1905-)* American Broadway stage composer.

Subotnick, Morton *(1933-)* American electronic-mixed media composer.

Sullivan, Sir Arthur *(1842-1900)* English composer.

Sullivan, Joe *(1906-)* American jazz pianist.

Suppe, Franz von *(1819-1895)* Austrian composer.

Surinach, Carlos *(1915-)* Spanish-American composer.

Swingle, Ward *(1927-)* American singer-arranger-Swingle Singers founder-leader.

Sydeman, William Jay *(1928-)* American composer.

Szell, George *(1897-1970)* Hungarian-American conductor.

Tt

Tailleferre, Germaine *(1892-1983)* French composer.

Tallis, Thomas *(1505-1585)* English religious choral music composer.

Tartini, Giuseppe *(1692-1770)* Italian violinist-composer-theorist.

Tatum, Art *(1910-1956)* Blind American jazz pianist.

Taylor, Cecil *(1933-)* American jazz pianist.

Taylor, Deems *(1885-1966)* American composer-musicologist.

Tchaikovsky, Peter Ilyich *(1840-1893)* Russian composer.

Tcherepnin, Alexander *(1899-1977)* Russian pianist-composer.

Teagarden, Jack *(1905-1964)* American jazz trombone player-singer.

Telemann, Georg Philipp *(1681-1767)* German composer.

Thomas, Michael Tilson *(1944-)* American conductor.

Thompson, Oscar *(1887-1945)* American lexicographer-music critic.

Thompson, Randall *(1899-1984)* American composer.

Thomson, Virgil *(1896-1989)* American composer-music critic.

Thorne, Francis *(1922-)* American composer.

Toch, Ernst *(1887-1964)* Austrian composer.

Tommasini, Vincenzo *(1878-1950)* Italian composer.

Torelli, Giuseppe *(1658-1709)* Italian violinist-composer.

Torme, Mel *(1925-)* American jazz singer-composer-author.

Toscanini, Arturo *(1867-1957)* Italian conductor.

Traubel, Helen *(1899-1972)* American operatic-pop soprano.

Travis, Roy *(1922-)* American composer.

Trumbauer, Frankie *(1900-1956)* American jazz saxophone player.

Tucker, Richard *(1913-1975)* American tenor.

Tucker, Sophie *(1884-1966)* Russian-American pop singer.

Tuckwell, Barry *(1931-)* Australian French horn player.

Tudor, David *(1926-)* American pianist-composer.

Turk, Daniel Gottlob *(1756-1813)* German composer.

Turner, Joe *(1911-1985)* American blues singer.

Uu

Ussachevsky, Vladimir *(1911-1990)* Russian-American electronic music composer.

Vv

Vallee, Rudy *(1901-1986)* American pop singer-saxophone player-bandleader-actor.

Varese, Edgard *(1883-1965)* French-American composer.

Vaughan, Sarah *(1924-1990)* American jazz singer-pianist.

Vaughan Williams, Ralph *(1872-1958)* English composer.

Venuti, Joe *(1904-1978)* American jazz violinist-bandleader.

Verdi, Giuseppe *(1813-1901)* Italian opera composer.

Villa-Lobos, Heitor *(1887-1959)* Brazilian composer.

Vincent, John *(1902-1977)* American composer.

Viotti, Giovanni Battista *(1775-1824)* Italian violinist-composer.

Vivaldi, Antonio *(1678-1741)* Italian composer.

Vogler, Georg Joseph *(1749-1814)* German composer-theorist.

Ww

Wagner, Joseph Frederick *(1900-1974)* American composer.

Wagner, Richard *(1813-1883)* German composer.

Wallenstein, Alfred F. *(1898-1983)* American cellist-conductor.

Waller, Thomas "Fats" *(1904-1943)* American jazz pianist-singer-songwriter.

Walter, Bruno *(1876-1962)* German conductor.

Walton, Sir William *(1902-1983)* English composer.

Ward, Robert *(1917-)* American composer.

Ward-Steinman, David *(1936-)* American composer.

Warfield, William *(1920-)* American baritone-pedagogue.

Waring, Fred *(1900-1984)* American choral conductor-pedagogue.

Warwick, Dionne *(1941-)* American pop singer-pianist.

Washington, Dinah *(1924-1963)* American blues singer-pianist.

Waters, Ethel *(1896-1977)* American singer-actress.

Watts, Andre *(1946-)* American pianist.

Weber, Carl Maria von *(1786-1826)* German opera composer.

Webern, Anton von *(1883-1945)* Austrian serial composer.

Weill, Kurt *(1900-1950)* German-American composer.

Weinberger, Jaromire *(1896-1967)* Czech opera composer.

Weiner, Lazar *(1897-1982)* Russian-American composer.

Weingartner, Felix *(1863-1942)* Austrian conductor.

Weisgall, Hugo *(1912-)* American composer.

Welk, Lawrence *(1903-1992)* American accordion player-bandleader.

Whiteman, Paul *(1890-1967)* American commercial conductor.

Wilder, Alex *(1907-1980)* American composer-songwriter-author.

Willan, Healey *(1880-1968)* Canadian composer.

Williams, Hank *(1923-1953)* American country music singer-guitarist-songwriter

Williams, Joe *(1918-)* American blues singer.

Williams, John M. *(1884-1974)* American pianist.

Williams, Mary Lou *(1910-1981)* American jazz pianist-composer-pedagogue.

Williams, Tex *(1917-1985)* American country and western singer.

Willson, Meredith *(1902-1984)* American composer-lyricist-writer.

Wilson, Olly *(1937-)* American composer.

Wilson, Teddy *(1912-1986)* American jazz pianist.

Winding, Kai *(1922-1983)* Danish-American jazz trombone player.

Wolf, Hugo *(1860-1903)* Austrian lieder composer.

Wolpe, Stefan *(1902-1972)* German-American composer-pedagogue.

Wonder, Stevie *(1951-)* Blind American singer-composer-keyboardist.

Wuorinen, Charles *(1938-)* American composer.

Xx

Xenakis, Iannis *(1922-)* Rumanian-Greek composer.

Yy

Young, La Monte *(1935-)* American composer.

Young, Lester *(1909-1959)* American jazz tenor saxophone player.

Zz

Zador, Eugen *(1894-1977)* Hungarian-American composer.

Zappa, Frank *(1940-1993)* American rock singer-guitarist-composer.

Zimbalist, Efrem *(1889-1985)* Russian-American violinist-pedagogue.

Zimmermann, Bernd-Alois *(1918-1970)* German composer.

Zingarelli, Niccolo Antonio *(1752-1837)* Neapolitan composer.

Zukofsky, Paul *(1943-)* American violinist.

THEORY

TEMPO AND EXPRESSION TERMS

Tempo (Metronome) Indications

Grave *(It.)* The slowest musical tempo; very slow and solemn.

Largo *(It.)* A slow, broad tempo, almost as slow as grave.

Larghetto *(It.)* A tempo not quite as slow as largo.

Adagio *(It.)* A slow tempo, slower than andante, but not so slow as largo.

Adagietto *(It.)* A tempo somewhat less slow than adagio, or a short piece in adagio tempo.

Lento *(It.)* A slow tempo, usually between adagio and andante.

Andante *(It.)* A slow, even tempo; literally, "going."

Andantino *(It.)* A little less slow than andante.

Moderato *(It.)* Moderate tempo, between andantino and allegretto.

Allegretto *(It.)* Light, cheerful; like allegro, but a little less fast.

Allegro *(It.)* Quick, lively; rapid and cheerful.

Presto *(It.)* Very rapidly; quicker than any tempo except prestissimo.

Prestissimo *(It.)* Extremely fast; as fast as possible. The quickest tempo in music.

Additional Tempo Indications

Accelerando *(It.)* Accelerating; increasing the speed.

Affretando *(It.)* Hurrying, quickening the tempo.

A tempo *(It.)* In the original speed.

Comodo *(It.)* Quietly, easily, conveniently.

Con moto *(It.)* With motion; rather quick.

L'istesso tempo *(It.)* In the same tempo as the previous section.

Meno mosso *(It.)* Less movement, slower.

Mosso *(It.)* Movement, motion, speed.

Moto *(It.)* Motion, movement.

Piu Mosso *(It.)* More motion, quicker.

Rallentando *(It.)* Making the tempo gradually slower.

Ritardando *(It.)* Retarding, delaying the time gradually.

Ritenuto *(It.)* Retained, kept back; more slowly.

Rubato *(It.)* A style of playing in which one note may be extended at the expense of another, for the purposes of expression.

Stringendo *(It.)* Hurrying, accelerating the tempo.

Tempo Primo *(It.)* First, or original, tempo.

Vivace *(It.)* A brisk, animated tempo.

Vivo *(It.)* Lively, animated.

Tempo and Dynamic Indications

Allargando *(It.)* Growing broad; slower.

Calando *(It.)* Becoming softer and slower.

Morendo *(It.)* Dying away, gradually.

Perdendosi *(It.)* Decreasing in power, dying away.

Dynamic Indications

Crescendo *(It.)* A gradual increase in power.

Decrescendo *(It.)* Gradually diminishing the power.

Diminuendo *(It.)* Gradually diminished in power.

Forte *(It.)* Loud, strong. Abbreviated to *f*.

Fortepiano *(It.)* Attack loudly; sustain softly.

Fortissimo *(It.)* Very loud. Abbreviated to *ff*.

Mezzo forte *(It.)* Moderately loud. Abbreviated to *mf*

Mezzo piano *(It.)* Moderately soft. Abbreviated to *mp*

Piano *(It.)* Soft Abbreviated to *p*.

Pianissimo *(It.)* Very soft. Abbreviated to *pp*.

Expression Indications

Affetto *(It.)* Sorrowfully, mournfully.

Affettuoso *(It.)* With tender expression.

Amabile *(It.)* Amiable, graceful, gentle.

Amorevole *(It.)* Loving, gentle.

Animato *(It.)* Animated; with spirit.

Animo *(It.)* Spirit.

Appassionato *(It.)* Passionate, intense.

Bravura *(It.)* Spirit, skill, requiring dexterity.

Brillante *(It.)* Brilliant, sparkling.

Brio *(It.)* Sprightliness, spirit.

Calmo *(It.)* Calm; tranquil.

Caloroso *(It.)* Warm, animated.

Cantabile *(It.)* In a singing style, smoothly.

Capriccioso *(It.)* Capriciously, fancifully.

Deciso *(It.)* Boldly, decidedly.

Dolce *(It.)* Sweetly.

Doloroso *(It.)* Sadly, sorrowfully.

Expressione *(It.)* Expression.

Espressivo *(It.)* Expressive.

Forza *(It.)* Force, power.

Fuoco *(It.)* Fire, passion.

Furioso *(It.)* Furious, vehement.

Gaio *(It.)* Gay.

Giocoso *(It.)* Merry, humorous.

Gioviale *(It.)* Jovial.

Grazioso *(It.)* Graceful.

Maestoso *(It.)* Majestic, stately.

Marcia *(It.)* March.

Marziale *(It.)* Martial.

Misterioso *(It.)* Mysteriously.

Piangendo *(It.)* Plaintively, sorrowfully.

Pomposo *(It.)* Pompous.

Ponderoso *(It.)* Ponderous; strongly marked.

Precisione *(It.)* Precision, exactness.

Risoluto *(It.)* Resolute, hold.

Scherzando *(It.)* Jestingly.

Scherzo *(It.)* A jest, or play. A piece in lively tempo and jesting style.

Secco *(It.)* Unornamented.

Semplice *(It.)* Simple, in a pure style.

Sentimentale *(It.)* Sentimental.

Sentimento *(It.)* Sentiment.

Sereno *(It.)* Serene; tranquil.

Serioso *(It.)* Gravely, seriously.

Spirito *(It.)* Spirit; fire; energy.

Spiritoso *(It.)* Spirited.

Teneramente *(It.)* Tenderly; delicately.

Tranquillo *(It.)* Tranquil, calm.

NOTATION

Simple			Compound	
NOTES		**RESTS**	**NOTES**	**RES**
=	Double Whole (Breve)	▪	=.	Dotted Double Whole (Dotted Breve)
o	Whole (Semi-Breve)	▬	o.	Dotted Whole
♩	Half (Minim)	▬	♩.	Dotted Half
♩	Quarter (Crotchet)	‿	♩.	Dotted Quarter
♪	Eight (Quaver)	߬	♪.	Dotted Eight
♪	Sixteenth (Semiquaver)	߬	♪.	Dotted Sixteenth
♪	Thirty-Second (Demisemi-quaver)	߬	♪.	Dotted Thirty-Second
♪	Sixty-Fourth (Hemidemi-semiquaver)	߬	♪.	Dotted Sixty fourth

SIGNS

Pitch

(♩)	Note head	♮	Natural
(♩)	Note stem	x	Double sharp
♪	Note flag	♭♭	Double flat
♪	Grace note	M	Major chord
8va	All' ottava	m (-)	Minor chord
8va basso	All' ottava	d (o)	Diminished chord
♯	Sharp	∅	Half-diminished 7th chord
♭	Flat	A (+)	Augmented chord

Dynamic

pp or *ppp*	Pianissimo	*ff* or *fff*	Fortissimo
p	Piano	*f*	Forte
mp	Mezzopiano	*mf*	Mezzoforte
>	Decrescendo *(Decr.)*	<	Crescendo *(Cresc.)*
>	Diminuendo *(Dim.)*	*sf*	Sforzato
<>	Messa Di Voce	*fp*	Forte-Piano

Rhythmic

¢	Alla Breve	⌒	Fermata (Hold)
$\frac{2}{4}$	Meter Signature	//	Pause
Acc.	Accelerando	*Rit.*	Ritardando

Performance

>∧	Accents	▭	Pesante, impressive
ṗ̄	Stressed and Sustained	[	To be played with same finger or hand
,	Breath mark	∧	Organ music, play with toes
ṗ	Staccato	∪	Organ music, play with heel
▼	Intense staccato	⌐ ⌐	Organ music, alternately heel and toe of same foot
Portato		⋅—▸	Change toes on organ pedal
⌒	Slur		Slide same toe to next note
⁓	Accented and sustained	Trill	
		‖:	Repeat sign

190

	Right Hand	o	Harmonic
	Left Hand		Arpeggio or Arpeggiando
	Tie		Tremolo or Roll
	Repeated notes		Tremolo legato
	Repeated notes	⁄	Measure repeat sign
	Continuation of Trill	⌐ bis	Repeat everything under bracket
....	Continuation of Octave mark	{	Bracket (Brace)
	Arpeggio — broken chord		A Stave
Ped.	Loud pedal on piano	𝄋 ⊕	Segno
*	Release the pedal		(Sign from which repeat is made)
∨	Marking exactly the points of depressing and releasing the pedal	ten.	Tenuto
⊓	Down Bow	V.S.	Volti subito Turn page quickly
V	Up Bow		Repeat

191

SIMPLE METERS

DUPLE	TRIPLE	QUADRUPLE
$\frac{2}{2}$ = (2 / 𝅗𝅥)	$\frac{3}{2}$ = (3 / 𝅗𝅥)	$\frac{4}{2}$ = (4 / 𝅗𝅥)
$\frac{2}{4}$ = (2 / ♩)	$\frac{3}{4}$ = (3 / ♩)	$\frac{4}{4}$ = (4 / ♩)
$\frac{2}{8}$ = (2 / ♪)	$\frac{3}{8}$ = (3 / ♪)	$\frac{4}{8}$ = (4 / ♪)
$\frac{2}{16}$ = (2 / ♬)	$\frac{3}{16}$ = (3 / ♬)	$\frac{4}{16}$ = (4 / ♬)

COMPOUND METERS

DUPLE	TRIPLE	QUADRUPLE
$\frac{6}{4}$ = (2 / 𝅗𝅥.)	$\frac{9}{4}$ = (3 / 𝅗𝅥.)	$\frac{12}{4}$ = (4 / 𝅗𝅥.)
$\frac{6}{8}$ = (2 / ♩.)	$\frac{9}{8}$ = (3 / ♩.)	$\frac{12}{8}$ = (4 / ♩.)
$\frac{6}{16}$ = (2 / ♪.)	$\frac{9}{16}$ = (3 / ♪.)	$\frac{12}{16}$ = (4 / ♪.)

KEY SIGNATURES

C Major
A minor

G Major   D Major   A Major
E minor   B minor   F♯ minor

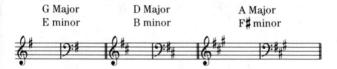

E Major   B Major
C♯ minor   G♯ minor

F♯ Major   C♯ Major
D♯ minor   A♯ minor

ORDER OF SHARPS AND FLATS

OCTAVE REGISTERS

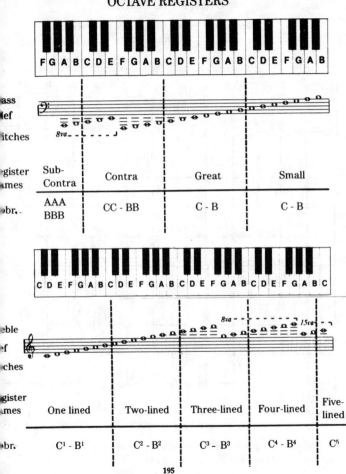

	Sub-Contra	Contra	Great	Small
Register names				
Abbr.	AAA BBB	CC - BB	C - B	C - B

	One lined	Two-lined	Three-lined	Four-lined	Five-lined
Register names					
Abbr.	$C^1 - B^1$	$C^2 - B^2$	$C^3 - B^3$	$C^4 - B^4$	C^5

OVERTONE SERIES

Harmonics Generated by a Fundamental
(Great C*)

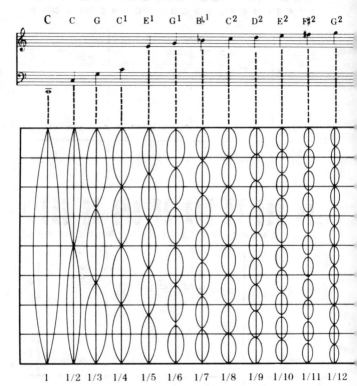

* Harmonics are generated by any given note serving as the fundamental producing the same intervallic relationship.

INTERVALS

NAMES	ABBREVIATIONS	INVERSIONS

NAMES	ABBREVIATIONS
Perfect	P
Prime	p
Major	M
Minor	m
Augmented	A
Diminished	D
Doubly Augmented	DA
Doubly Diminished	Dd

INVERSIONS

(P (A) 5
m2⎯⎯M6
m3⎯⎯M7
P (p) 4

Perfect 5th, when
inverted, becomes
Perfect 4th, etc.

EXPANSION AND CONTRACTION OF INTERVALS

Smaller   Larger

Double diminished Dd	diminished d	minor m / Major M — Perfect P		Augmented A	Doubly Augmented DA

INTERVAL, ENHARMONIC

197

INTERVALS

Diatonic Interval Construction

Major

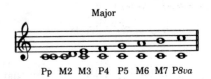

Pp M2 M3 P4 P5 M6 M7 P8*va*

Minor

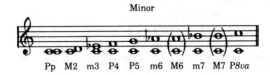

Pp M2 m3 P4 P5 m6 M6 m7 M7 P8*va*

EXAMPLES OF TYPES OF INTERVALS

Perfect

Pp Ap DAp dp Ddp   P4 A4 DA4 d4 Dd4

P5 A5 DA5 d5 Dd5   P8 A8 DA8 d8 Dd8

Major

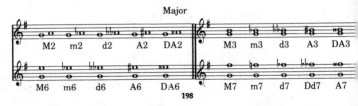

M2 m2 d2 A2 DA2   M3 m3 d3 A3 DA3

M6 m6 d6 A6 DA6   M7 m7 d7 Dd7 A7

SCALES AND MODES *

Major (Ionian)   Ascending   Descending

Minor (Pure or Natural) (Aeolian)

Minor (Harmonic)

Minor (Melodic)

Chromatic

Dorian

Phrygian

Lydian Major

Mixolydian

⌣ = ½ Step   ⋀ = 1 ½ Steps

* In each example the starting note "C" was chosen arbitrarily- The scales or modes may
begin on any note encompassing one octave ascending and descending.

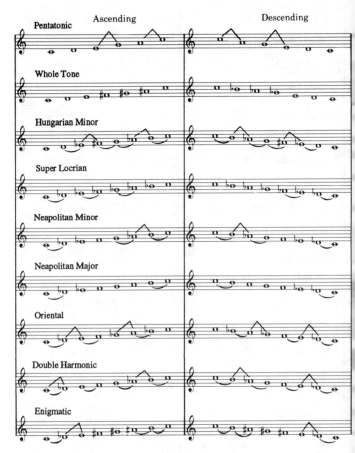

CLEFS

Indicating the relative position of "Middle C"

French Violin Clef   Treble Clef   Soprano Clef

Mezzo-Soprano Clef   Alto Clef   Tenor Clef

Baritone Clef   Baritone Clef   Bass Clef   Sub-Bass Clef

CHORD TYPES

Type	Abbreviation	Functional Nomenclature	Example
Major	M	CM	
minor	m	Cm C-	
diminished	d	C♯° C♯dim.	

ugmented	A	C Aug. C+ C (+5), C#5	
ajor-minor eventh	Mm7	C7	
ajor-Major eventh	m7	CM7 Cmaj7	
inor-minor venth (minor-seventh)	mm7	C-7 Cm7, Cmin. 7	
inor-Major eventh	mM7	Cmin. (Maj7) C-(Maj7)	
iminished-minor eventh	dm7	C#7	
iminished-diminished eventh (diminished-seventh)	d7	C#°7 C# (dim. 7)	
ugmented-major eventh	AM7	C + (7) C Aug. (7)	
ugmented-minor eventh	Am7	C + (Maj. 7) C Aug. (Maj. 7)	

CHORD INVERSIONS

FUNDAMENTAL POSITION OF TRIADS

C: I

FIRST INVERSION CHORD

C: V^6

SECOND INVERSION CHORD

C: V$^6_4$

SEVENTH CHORD

C: I⁷

FIRST INVERSION SEVENTH CHORD

C: V_5^6

SECOND INVERSION SEVENTH CHORD

C: V_3^4

THIRD INVERSION SEVENTH CHORD

C: V_2^4

SIXTH CHORDS

FRENCH SIXTH CHORD

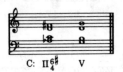

C: II$^{6\sharp}_{4}$ V

GERMAN SIXTH CHORD

C: IV$^{6\sharp}_{5}$ V

ITALIAN SIXTH CHORD

C: IV 6$\sharp$ V

NEAPOLITAN SIXTH CHORD

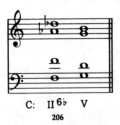

C: II $^{6\flat}$ V

JAZZ CHORD TYPES
Major Chords

Major triad
C

Major triad with added sixth
C6

Major triad with added sixth and ninth
C6 9

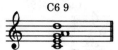

Major triad with added ninth only
C (add 9)

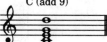

Dominant seventh
C7

Dominant ninth
C9

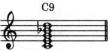

Dominant eleventh
C11

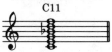

Dominant thirteenth
C13

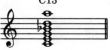

Major seventh
Cmaj7

Major ninth
Cmaj9

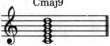

JAZZ CHORD TYPES
Minor Chords

Minor triad
Cmi

Minor triad
with added sixth
Cmi6

Minor triad
with added sixth and ninth
Cmi6 9

Minor triad
with added ninth only
Cmi (add 9)

Minor seventh
Cmi7

Minor ninth
Cmi9

Minor eleventh
Cmi11

Minor thirteenth
Cmi13

Minor triad
with major seventh
Cmi (maj7)

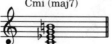

Minor ninth
with major seventh
Cmi9 (maj7)

Jazz Chord Types
Diminished Chords

Diminished triad
Dmi (♭5)

Diminished seventh
D°

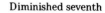

Augmented Chords
Augmented triad

C +

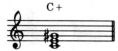

Augmented dominant seventh
C + 7

Augmented dominant seventh and ninth
C + 9

Augmented major seventh
C + (maj7)

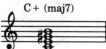

Augmented major seventh and ninth
C + 9 (maj7)

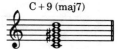

Augmented minor triad
Cmi +

Augmented minor triad and minor seventh
Cmi + 7

Jazz Chord Types
Flat Fifths

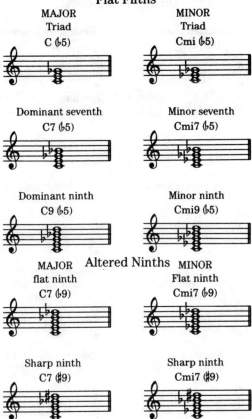

MAJOR
Triad
C (♭5)

MINOR
Triad
Cmi (♭5)

Dominant seventh
C7 (♭5)

Minor seventh
Cmi7 (♭5)

Dominant ninth
C9 (♭5)

Minor ninth
Cmi9 (♭5)

MAJOR   Altered Ninths   MINOR

flat ninth
C7 (♭9)

Flat ninth
Cmi7 (♭9)

Sharp ninth
C7 (♯9)

Sharp ninth
Cmi7 (♯9)

JAZZ CHORD TYPES
Altered Fifths and Ninths Combined

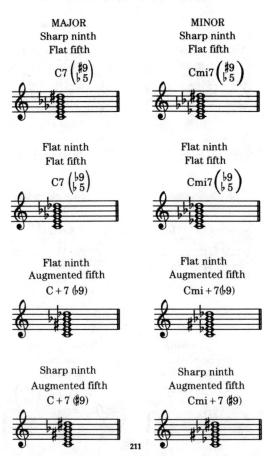

MAJOR
Sharp ninth
Flat fifth

C7 $\begin{pmatrix} \sharp 9 \\ \flat 5 \end{pmatrix}$

MINOR
Sharp ninth
Flat fifth

Cmi7 $\begin{pmatrix} \sharp 9 \\ \flat 5 \end{pmatrix}$

Flat ninth
Flat fifth

C7 $\begin{pmatrix} \flat 9 \\ \flat 5 \end{pmatrix}$

Flat ninth
Flat fifth

Cmi7 $\begin{pmatrix} \flat 9 \\ \flat 5 \end{pmatrix}$

Flat ninth
Augmented fifth

C + 7 ($\flat$9)

Flat ninth
Augmented fifth

Cmi + 7($\flat$9)

Sharp ninth
Augmented fifth

C + 7 ($\sharp$9)

Sharp ninth
Augmented fifth

Cmi + 7 ($\sharp$9)

JAZZ CHORD TYPES
Altered Elevenths

MAJOR
Sharp eleventh
Augmented eleventh

C9 (♯11)

MINOR
Sharp eleventh
Augmented eleventh

Cmi9 (♯11)

Sharp eleventh
Flat ninth

C7 $\left(\begin{smallmatrix}♯11\\♭9\end{smallmatrix}\right)$

Sharp eleventh
Flat ninth

Cmi7 $\left(\begin{smallmatrix}♯11\\♭5\end{smallmatrix}\right)$

Sharp eleventh
Flat ninth
Augmented fifth

C + 7 $\left(\begin{smallmatrix}♯11\\♭9\end{smallmatrix}\right)$

Sharp eleventh
Flat ninth
Augmented fifth

Cmi + 7 $\left(\begin{smallmatrix}♯11\\♭9\end{smallmatrix}\right)$

JAZZ ARTICULATION

The shake-a variation of the tone upwards-much like trill.

Lip trill-similar to shake but slower and with more lip control

Wide lip trill-same as above except slower and with a wider interval.

The Flip-sound note, raise pitch, drop into following note (done with lip on brass).

The smear-slide into mute from below and reach current pitch just before most note — do not rob preceding note.

Du - false or muffled note.

Wah-full tone-not muffled.

The doit — sound note then gliss upwards from one to five stieps.

Short gliss up-slide into note from below (one to three steps).

Long gliss up-same as short gliss with longer entrance.

Short gliss down-the reverse of the short gliss up.

Long gliss down - the reverse of the long gliss up.

Short lift-enter note via cromatic or distonic scale starting about a third below.

Long lift-same as above with longer entrance.

Short spill-rapid diatonic or chromatic drop - the reverse of the short lift.

Long spill - same as above with longer exit.

The plop-a rapid slide down harmonically or diatonically before sounding note.

Indefinite sound - deadened tone - indefinite pitch.

NONHARMONIC TONES

MUSICAL ORNAMENTS

Written **Played**

Nachschlag preceded by a dotted note

Nachschlag followed by a repeated note

Nachschlag preceded by a rest

Short Italian Acciaccatura

Short German Vorschlag

Italian Appoggiatura

Pralltriller

MUSICAL ORNAMENTS

Written   Played

Mordent

Inverted Mordent

Inverted Turn

Turn with
Nachschlag Group

Quintuplet Turn

Trill on lower
auxiliary

Trill on upper
auxiliary

Quintuplet Trill

ARTIFICIAL RHYTHMIC GROUPINGS

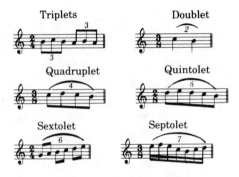

Large Group

CONDUCTING FRAMES

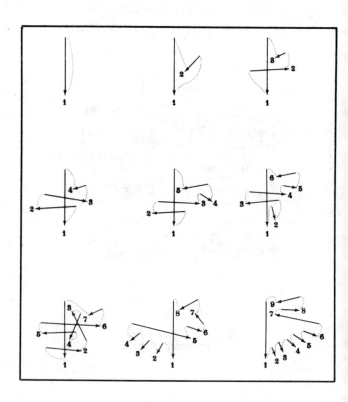

THE NEW BELWIN DICTIONARIES
researched and edited by William Lee

The Belwin Dictionary of Music
Unabridged, 9" x 12"
__ (EL 03945) Book $9.95
__ (EL 03945MAC) Book w/MAC disk $14.95
__ (EL 03945IBM) Book w/IBM disk $14.95
__ (EL 03945MDSK) MAC disk only $5.95
__ (EL 03945IDSK) IBM disk only $5.95
Abridged, Pocket Size: 4¼" x 5½"
__ (EL 03946) Book $4.95
A comprehensive presentation of basic and traditional terminology, biographies, history and literature.

Music in the 21st Century: The New Language
Unabridged, 9" x 12"
__ (EL 03947) Book $9.95
__ (EL 03947MAC) Book w/MAC disk $14.95
__ (EL 03947IBM) Book w/IBM disk $14.95
__ (EL 03947MDSK) MAC disk only $5.95
__ (EL 03947IDSK) IBM disk only $5.95
Abridged, Pocket Size: 4¼" x 5½"
__ (EL 03948) Book $4.95
For those who want or need to understand the evolution of music terminology as it is happening on a daily basis.

Belwin Dictionary of Music plus Music in the 21st Century

__ (EL 03956CDR) CD-ROM disk only $12.95
__ (EL 03956CDSK) CD-ROM disk plus both unabridged 9" x 12" volumes $29.95